Hour Of The Cat

Also by Jean DeWeese
THE DOLL WITH OPAL EYES

And with Robert Coulson
NOW YOU SEE IT/HIM/THEM . . .
CHARLES FORT NEVER MENTIONED WOMBATS

Hour Of The Cat

JEAN DEWEESE

DOUBLEDAY & COMPANY, INC.

GARDEN CITY, NEW YORK

1980

All of the characters in this book
are fictitious, and any resemblance
to actual persons, living or dead,
is purely coincidental.

Library of Congress Cataloging in Publication Data
DeWeese, Gene.
   Hour of the cat.
   I. Title.
PZ4.D5155Ho [PS3554.E929]   813'.5'4
ISBN: 0-385-12098-2
Library of Congress Catalog Card Number 79-7194

80000175

For Bev, who's right a disconcerting percentage of the time.

Hour Of The Cat

The plan sprang into his mind, complete and full-formed, the instant he saw her.

It was as if he were reborn in that one moment of brilliant insight. After an eternity of bitterness and frustration, his life suddenly had purpose. He no longer existed only in that tortured limbo into which Sandra's brutal murder had cast him. At last he was able to act! And act he did, unlike that cowardly, temporizing fool who had plagued him all those endless years!

And once he began, as each new action inexorably followed the last, he knew that, no matter what obstacles were thrown in his path, no matter who opposed him, he would eventually succeed, and justice, so long delayed, would finally be served.

Chapter 1

Valerie Hamilton swore under her breath as, once again, her fingers refused to pay proper attention to her orders and form a decent E^7 chord. As usual, it was her little finger that was the culprit. She had long ago developed fairly good control over the others, but that one still occasionally rebelled, simply refusing to cooperate on anything new. And tonight it seemed to have a mind of its own, settling on whatever string or fret it felt like, whether it was part of the chord she wanted or not.

Irritably, Val dropped the guitar on the couch next to her and stretched her arms out in front of her, alternately straightening and curling her fingers as tightly as she could. She had better just drop the project for the evening. Learning a new song—particularly one like "Sam Hall," which she had loved ever since she'd heard Josh White's raucous recording several years before—was supposed to be fun, but her little finger was rapidly turning it into work.

Or maybe the phone calls were the cause of her miserable coordination this particular evening. There had been at least a half dozen in the two hours since she'd come home from the library, all congratulating her on her nonexistent engagement to Martin Forster, as announced in the *Hazleton Tribune* society page that afternoon. After the first couple of calls, Val had her response memorized: "The item in the *Tribune* is wrong. I don't know *where* they got their information, but I am *not* engaged—not to Mr. Forster or to anyone else." Still, the constant interruptions and her own puzzlement as to who had placed the item—and why—were not conducive to anything that required the least bit of concentration.

But maybe it's just as well, she thought with a sudden grin. She'd never dare do "Sam"—at least not the unexpurgated version—at tomorrow night's fund-raising party anyway. Most of the people there would be relatively open-minded, but she didn't think Hazleton was quite ready for "Sam" and his exuberant gallows profanity, at least not from the lips of Hazleton's brand new, green-eyed librarian. In the three months she had been in Hazleton, she had found that, despite all logic, there were still people who believed that librarians, particularly librarians as petite—barely five feet—and innocent looking as Valerie Hamilton, should not even be aware of such language, let alone stoop to using it occasionally.

Shaking her head, she glanced at her watch. Almost nine-thirty, she noticed, frowning as she remembered she hadn't checked the back door for Muldoon lately. It was already past time for that overly hairy feline to be getting back from his after-supper outing. Springing to her feet, she hurried along the hall past her tiny office on the right and bedroom on the left. In the kitchen, her low-heeled shoes beat a quick rhythm on the linoleum as she went through, pausing only to snap on the light, grimace at the sink half full of guilt-inducing, unwashed dishes, and imagine the face her mother would make if she could see them. A second later she stepped outside the back door and snapped on the yard light, mounted high up on the wall to her right. The brisk, autumnlike air felt good after the summery mugginess of only a dozen hours before, and for a moment she simply stood on the small back step, enjoying the feel of the light breeze on her face, enjoying the sound it made as it rustled through the tall bushes that lined both sides of the yard.

No wonder he doesn't want to come in, she thought. If I were a cat, I wouldn't want to either.

"Muldoon?" she called, and then listened. After a second, she whistled, a shrill blast that carried for at least half a block. A dog somewhere in the alley—probably Manfred, the Hyatts' collie—barked, but that was the only response. Again she whistled, keeping an intermittent eye on the corner of the garage, around which Muldoon usually made his appearance after his neighborhood forays.

But there was nothing.

She was just flipping off the light and turning to go back inside when the phone rang again. Automatically she started toward it, but she stopped after a couple of steps. It was just going to be someone else offering congratulations on her engagement, and she didn't really feel like explaining the mistake yet another time. On the other hand, she knew that she wouldn't be able to listen to the phone ringing for any length of time without answering it.

So I won't listen, she thought abruptly.

Turning to the kitchen counter, she snatched up the metal can half full of Muldoon's favorite snack and was hurrying out the door by the time the next jangling ring began. Slipping past her four-year-old Gremlin in the darkened garage, she raised the clanking metal garage door and emerged into the alley. Manfred, barking a greeting, bounded out of a brightly lighted garage a couple houses toward the center of the block as Val lowered the door noisily behind her. The jangling of the phone was reduced to a distant tinkling.

"Freddie, knock it off!" Joe Hyatt's gruff voice came from the open garage, and then Joe himself, a paint sprayer in one rawboned hand, stepped into the alley. His coveralls were a mixture of grease and paint of a half-dozen different colors. Hyatt, in his sixties now, had been sheriff until he'd retired three or four years ago, and now he and one of his sons, whenever they felt like it, operated a small body shop out of Hyatt's garage.

"Hi, Val," he called as he spotted her walking slowly in his direction. Then his eyes went to Muldoon's snack can, already a familiar sight in the neighborhood. "Don't tell me your furry friend is missing again."

"More or less," Val said, giving the can a shake as she neared Hyatt and the tail-wagging Manfred. The can rattled loudly, like a tin can full of pebbles, a sound that had been known to reel Muldoon in from the far end of the block and even distract him from stalking stray bugs and birds. "He's been gone a little longer than usual," she said, "and I thought I'd better check to be sure he hasn't gotten locked in someone's garage. It happened in Milwaukee a couple of times." She shrugged. "Besides, I felt like going for a walk." She didn't mention the phone, which had faded into silence by now.

"Haven't seen him around," Hyatt said, waving the paint sprayer at the cluttered interior of his garage. As usual, the bare bulb in the ceiling revealed a half-painted van and dozens of pieces that might or might not have been temporarily detached parts of the vehicle. "But if he shows up," Hyatt finished, "I'll shoo him in your direction."

"Thanks. He's probably just out enjoying the weather, like me."

She started to give the can another shake and listen for a response, but Hyatt said, hesitantly, "Incidentally, I saw about your engagement in the paper this evening." His voice sounded oddly somber, unlike the massive cheerfulness she'd gotten from everyone else.

She sighed. "Sorry, but it's not true. It was either a mistake or a joke."

Hyatt looked vaguely relieved, but then he frowned. "A joke? Who'd do a thing like that? Pretty rotten joke, if you ask me."

"Can't say I think much of it myself," Val said. "I've been spending half my time this evening telling people I'm not engaged and don't intend to be."

Hyatt shook his head. "A really rotten thing to do," he said again, and then added, "If whoever did it ever gives you any more trouble, you give me a call. You hear?" He waved the bulky paint sprayer menacingly.

"I will, but I can't imagine it ever coming to that. It's just a joke. A stupid one, but just a joke."

Hyatt nodded but said nothing as Val moved on down the alley, away from the light fanning out from the bare bulb in the ceiling of his garage. She glanced back once and saw him still looking after her. As she rattled the can and waved at him, he

blinked and hastily turned back to the garage and his interrupted painting.

The light on the pole at the far end of the alley was burned
out, she noticed as she moved on, alternately rattling the can
and listening at the garages. By the time she neared the end of
the alley, she had attracted two neighborhood cats, but not
Muldoon, and she was beginning to feel reluctantly uneasy. She
had felt silly at first, wandering down the alley more in an effort
to avoid the telephone than to actually look for Muldoon, but
now she was beginning to wonder. Normally, no matter what
the cat was doing, the rattling of that can would attract him instantly. And, so far as she knew, he'd never, in the three
months she had lived here, strayed entirely out of the block.

So where could he have gotten to? He'd been neutered two
years ago, so he certainly couldn't have gotten sidetracked *that*
way.

At the end of the alley, she gave the can one more series of
shakes and then stood silently, listening.

She spun around. Had that been something, in that last garage on the right? She listened again, but could hear nothing,
only the distant hissing of Joe Hyatt's paint sprayer.

As she turned to look back down the alley, she thought she
saw something move out of the corner of her eye, but when she
turned back, she saw that it was only a crumpled milk carton
that had fallen from someone's open garbage can.

And through a back window, visible across an unobstructed
back yard, a TV set flickered silently.

Shaking her head disgustedly at herself, she turned from the
alley and came out onto the sidewalk. She'd take a look at the
front yards as she went back, just to be sure.

But still there was nothing, not a sign of the cat, not on the
porches or in the darkened areas between the houses.

Despite herself, she quickened her pace as she neared her
own house. Involuntarily, her memory dredged up the story one
of the library aides in Milwaukee had told her last year. A
neighbor's dog had been shot by someone, apparently in broad
daylight, right in the middle of one of the city's "better" neigh-

borhoods. No one ever found out who did it or why. And there were, Val told herself uneasily, probably just as high a percentage of weirdos in small towns like Hazleton as there were in large cities.

As for Muldoon, he *was* friendly, probably too friendly for his own good at times. Almost anyone could pick him up, anywhere, anytime.

Swallowing, Val turned down the narrow concrete walkway that led between her house and the tall hedge that bordered the next yard. At least the phone had stopped ringing, she noted absently as she headed toward the oasis of light that was her back yard.

Suddenly, a figure loomed before her. It had stepped around the corner of the house from the back yard, and she could, in that first instant, see only a tall form silhouetted against the light.

The figure stopped abruptly, and Val realized that her heart was racing, adrenalin jolting through her as she jerked to a stop.

"Who—" she began, but another voice overlapped hers, cutting it off.

"Val? What are you doing out *here?*"

She let her breath out in a whoosh of relief as she recognized the voice and then, as her mind filled in the shadowed features, the figure itself.

"Martin! You scared the living— You scared me half to death!" she said, censoring herself. "What are *you* doing out here, lurking around my back yard?"

As always, Martin Forster's six-foot-plus, almost gaunt frame was clothed impeccably in a three-piece suit and tie. Despite the shadows that masked his lean features, Val was reasonably sure that they wore a matching look of faint disapproval, generated as his eyes moved over her own faded jeans and well-worn sweater. Though he sometimes made a valiant effort—mainly when, every few days, he renewed his repeatedly rejected invitation to her to have dinner with him—he apparently could not comprehend why anyone would willingly appear in public wearing anything so obviously unacceptable. There were times when she suspected he even disapproved of the slacks and pantsuits and ponchos she generally wore at the library. But that was his problem, not hers. It was hard enough finding practical clothes that would fit her hundred-pound, five-foot body without worrying about being the height of fashion or pleasing a casual, if persistent, acquaintance who—as had once been said of Adolphe Menjou—dressed like a Pierce Arrow.

"I was worried," Martin was saying. "I tried the front door, but no one answered. Then I saw the light in the back—"

"I was just out for a stroll, looking for Muldoon." She gave the can an illustrative rattle. "And avoiding the telephone. But I assume you've been getting your share of calls, too."

He looked at her blankly. "Calls? From whom?"

"From everyone. You mean no one's called to congratulate you on your engagement yet?"

"Oh." He shook his head, his face lengthening. "I haven't been home yet this evening. But that announcement in the *Tribune* is why I am here."

"Oh? You're going to explain what's going on? Good." She motioned with the can toward the back of the house. "Come on in a minute and tell me all about it. And if anyone calls, *you* can answer the phone since you obviously haven't been carrying your share of the load so far."

Without waiting for an answer, she edged past him on the narrow walk and made her way quickly to the back door. With a last look around the yard for Muldoon, she opened the door and stepped into the kitchen. As she was setting the can on the counter, Martin came in uneasily.

"I had nothing to do with it," he said.

"I never thought you did. You're not the practical-joking type. But I was hoping you might have an idea or two about who *did* do it."

"None. It must be someone's sick idea of a joke."

"I know that, but whose? One of your rowdy friends'?"

"Whoever is responsible for that announcement is no friend!" His voice was subdued but angry.

"You don't have any idea, then? No idea at all?"

"None. If I did . . ." His voice trailed off, and Val noticed his right hand half closing into a fist.

"Come on," she said lightly, "it's not *that* bad—unless you know something I don't." She looked at him curiously.

His lips parted as if he were about to speak, but then they clamped shut and he shook his head stubbornly. "It has nothing to do with you, whatever it is."

"*What* doesn't have anything to do with me? You *do* know something about it, don't you?"

"No. I merely came to apologize and to tell you I would insist that they run a prominent retraction in tomorrow's edition."

"What's to apologize for? Unless *you* put the item in in the first place. You didn't, did you?"

"Of course not! It's simply that— No, it's nothing. Just someone's asinine idea of a joke on me, that's all."

She watched him silently, trying to devise another line of questioning. But then, as she started to speak, there was a scratching at the basement door in the hall just outside the kitchen.

Frowning, she hurried into the hall and snapped on the light. She was just starting toward the basement door a few feet away when the phone rang.

"Get the phone, Martin," she called over her shoulder. "It's your turn to explain, okay? It's in the living room."

There was another scratching at the basement door as she hesitated, waiting for a reply. "Martin?"

Finally she heard him crossing the kitchen floor. He glanced at her uncertainly as he emerged into the hall.

"In the living room," she repeated, and then, without waiting to see what he did, hurried the remaining few feet to the basement door and snatched it open.

Muldoon, his huge, shaggy tail trailing behind him like a bushy cape, darted through the door and along the dozen feet of hallway into the kitchen. Martin glanced over his shoulder, hesitated as he saw the cat, but then turned back toward the living room as the phone continued to jangle insistently.

By the time Val reached the kitchen, Martin had picked up the receiver and Muldoon was pacing in a circle around the spot, near one end of the counter, where his food dish normally stood. As usual when he wanted either food or attention—which was most of the time, except when he was sleeping—he was repeatedly making a noise halfway between a purr and a muffled meow, not unlike, Val had always thought, a feline sonar beep. His gray and white fur didn't look any untidier than usual, but that wasn't saying much. Except for his face, which was reasonably neat and short haired, he was covered with enough fur for at least two cats, and it seemed to get longer the farther you looked from his head. His tail, now straight up, sprayed out in all directions until it looked as if it were wider than his body. Someone had once said it reminded him of those paper eucalyptus trees that Orson Bean used to make out of rolled up newspapers every few months on the various TV talk shows.

"All right, delinquent," Val said, taking the lid off the can of cat crunchies and dropping a few kernels of the hard, dry food into a small dish on the floor, "you probably think you're pretty cute, waiting till I go looking for you and then sneaking in through your own private entrance."

Muldoon, of course, paid no attention to the implied criticism and began crunching noisily, like someone cracking peanut brittle with his teeth. In any event, it was her own fault. She must have forgotten to close the "cat door," a tiny basement window which, unlike the other, larger ones, was hinged at the top and could, if left unlatched, be pushed open from the outside. She remembered leaving it open two or three mornings before, when Muldoon had overstayed his morning jaunt and hadn't gotten back by the time Val had to leave for the library.

She was putting the can of crunchies back in the large white cabinet full of cat food and cake mixes and other culinary odds and ends when Martin appeared in the door to the hall. He was frowning again.

"It's Daniel Richards," he said. "Do you want to talk to him?"

Dan Richards, like Martin Forster, was a lawyer and a junior partner in "Dennison and Associates," and if Val were ever going to be legitimately engaged to someone, it would more likely be to Dan than to Martin. Not that she was planning anything like that in the near future, but Dan at least was "her type," which meant he was about as unlike Martin as it was possible to be—except for height and profession, that is. Where Martin was dark, angular, addicted to three-piece suits, and possessed of a temperament to match, Dan was a dishwater blond, wore ties only when he had to make a court appearance, and was dignified only as a last resort.

For an instant, Val wondered if Dan could be behind the fake announcement, but she dismissed the idea immediately as she nodded to Martin and hurried past him toward the living room. Dan was not above a practical joke, but she couldn't imagine him pulling a pointless hoax like this one. An announcement of her engagement to *him,* maybe, just as a hint, but not this.

"Hi, Dan?" she said, snatching the receiver up from the coffee table and dropping precipitately onto the couch next to the guitar that still lay where she had left it. "Anything I can do for you?"

"You could start by telling me that the announcement of your engagement was greatly exaggerated, but considering who answered your phone just now . . . That was Marty, wasn't it?"

"It was, but don't worry about anything. That announcement was just someone's weird idea of a joke. I don't suppose *you* have any idea who's responsible?"

"Nary a one. But what about Marty? Did he have any ideas?"

She hesitated, glancing over her shoulder toward the hall door. Martin was nowhere in sight. He must still be in the kitchen.

"If he does have any ideas, he's not sharing them," Val said finally, keeping her voice low. "All he said was that he didn't have anything to do with it and that he'd get them to print a retraction tomorrow."

"That sounds like Marty, all business. He didn't even try to get you to make it come true? But that reminds me, tell your retracted fiancé to call Lichtenwalter this evening. He's at the Arlington, and he thought of something else after Marty left."

"Lichtenwalter? Isn't he the one that's going to build a shopping center out at the end of Walnut?"

"That's the guy. We've got the land all lined up, but we—or Marty, actually; he's been handling practically the whole thing —Marty has to convince the zoning board next week. Anyway, tell him to give Lichtenwalter a call. Tonight. He's going back to St. Louis first thing in the morning."

"Okay, I'll tell him. Or you can tell him yourself if you—"

"No, thanks. He's less likely to snarl at you than at me."

"Why should he snarl at anyone?"

"Don't ask me," Dan said, and she could hear the broad shrug in his voice. "But whatever the reason, he's been doing enough of it lately. But look, on a pleasanter topic, are you all set for tomorrow night?"

She grimaced as she glanced at the guitar next to her. "As ready as I'll ever be. I don't know why I ever let you talk me into this nonsense."

"*I* talked *you* into it? If that's any example of your veracity these days, I'll start thinking *you're* the one who put that announcement in the paper—just to make me jealous."

"If I did, I obviously wasted my time. It doesn't seem to be working. Now if you'll excuse me, I have to get back to my fiancé and my cat."

He laughed. "In that case, let me offer my congratulations. And I'll see you tomorrow evening if you've broken your engagement by then. And don't forget about Lichtenwalter."

The line went dead. Grinning and shaking her head, Val replaced the receiver and bounced to her feet.

In the hall, she met Muldoon as he came bounding out of the kitchen. Martin appeared in the door an instant later, lurching to a stop.

Val looked up at Martin, surprised by his rapid movement and sudden stop. Normally his motions were as deliberate and well coordinated as his suits.

"Dan said you should call Lichtenwalter tonight," she said. "Okay?" she added when he didn't respond. "You heard my message?"

He nodded distractedly, but his eyes followed the cat, who was pacing around Val's feet now, sonaring for a second helping of crunchies.

"Something wrong?" Val asked, frowning.

"There's something on its collar," Martin said, his voice barely audible.

Her frown deepened as she looked down. "What sort of something? I don't see—"

"Look more closely! I know I saw it!"

Puzzled, Val knelt down next to the cat, catching hold of him as he lowered his head and butted it against her foot and then toppled over like a bulldogged calf. It was his standard procedure when he wanted his stomach scratched, which was almost as often as he wanted fed.

As she parted the long, gray and white fur around his throat, she saw a piece of paper, folded several times until it was barely wider than the collar itself. It was held close against the collar, fastened by a single rubber band. She stood up, the folded paper in her fingers.

"What is it?" Martin asked sharply. He still stood motionless in the kitchen door a good two yards away, as if he were afraid to approach her.

"A piece of paper," she said, looking directly at him. "Do *you* know anything about this?"

He shook his head emphatically. "Of course not! What is it? What does it say?"

Val frowned and moved past him into the brightly lighted kitchen. She turned and looked up at him again. He swallowed nervously.

"You *do* know something about it," she said slowly.

Again he shook his head, and again he swallowed. "I don't," he said. "I honestly don't know a thing about it." He moistened his thin lips, and his eyes remained riveted to the paper. "I've never seen it before."

"Then why are you so—so blasted nervous? Look, Martin, level with me before you start really scaring me, all right? Is this all part of some elaborate joke? This and the engagement?"

"No!" The word erupted from him. "Now please, open it! Then perhaps we'll have some idea of what is happening!"

Still watching Martin suspiciously, Val began to unfold the paper. After a second, when it was half open, she saw that it was part of a page torn from a spiral notebook.

The letters appeared slowly as she unrolled. At first, she thought only how neatly formed the letters—all capitals—were. It was as if they had been done using a draftsman's lettering guide. There were faint smudges, however, and slight irregularities, as if the guide had slipped now and then. And the letters were done with a ballpoint, not a drafting pen.

Then, abruptly, as the unfolding was completed and her eyes focussed on the entire sheet, the letters came together into words, and a chill settled over her back like a cloak. Softly, her lips formed the words: " 'Marry him if you dare. You will be lucky to survive the honeymoon.' "

An instant later Martin snatched the paper from her hands so abruptly that it tore, leaving a ragged corner to flutter to the floor as she belatedly released her grip. For a long time Martin stood silently, his eyes staring unbelievingly at the neatly printed words. The only sound was from Muldoon, who had followed Val back into the kitchen and was once again sonaring around his empty dish.

Martin's face was grim. For a moment it looked as if he were going to crumple the note in his hands, but instead he folded it carefully into quarters and put it into the inside pocket of his jacket.

But his hands were shaking, and Val couldn't tell if it was from anger or from fear.

He watched as Forster, still trembling, made his way from the house. The first message, he knew, was in Forster's pocket— and in his mind!

Forster had recognized it, of that he was positive. But was that enough? Would he still somehow manage to blind himself to reality?

But no! This time he would not be allowed to close his eyes to the truth! He would not be allowed to hide his head in the sands of self-deception! This time the truth would be forced upon him! This time Sandra would not—

His thoughts blurred as Sandra's image once again forced its way into his mind. He felt his throat tighten, threatening to cut off his breath. His vision blurred as the tears once again began to flow, tears not only of bitterness and sorrow but of futile anger.

With an effort that almost brought a physical cry of anguish from his throat, he forced the images and the agony of the past from his mind. He could not afford such luxuries now. He could afford only to continue with the plan. He could afford only to look to the future, to the ever strengthening prospect of justice and redemption.

Chapter 2

Martin had been positive in his reassurances that the entire "joke" was directed at him rather than at Val, but he had refused—or been unable—to explain how he knew this. And then, as if to underscore his refusal and his uneasiness, he stalked out of the house. Val watched through the living-room window next to the small front porch as he fumbled with his keys, almost dropping them in the street before getting his gray, year-old Cadillac unlocked. He finally managed to get in and get it started, though, and he tore off down the street like the worst hot rodder. It might well be "only a joke," as Martin had emphasized repeatedly, but it was obviously one that did not amuse him.

As she turned from the window and flopped unceremoniously onto the couch along the opposite wall, she thought briefly of calling Dan and seeing what he had to say about this uncharacteristic behavior of his law partner, but she resisted the temptation. In the first place, even on the remote chance that it *wasn't* a joke, she was in no particular danger since she had no intention in the world of even dating Martin, let alone marrying him. In the second place, there was nothing either she or Dan could do about it, so all they would do would be waste a lot of time in pointless speculation. And she had better things to do than that. The stack of books she had lugged home from the library three days ago, for instance.

Brushing her loosely curling, dark brown hair back from her forehead with one hand, she grabbed the top book from the stack of half a dozen on the coffee table in front of the couch. She really should get at least this one back to the library pretty soon. There weren't any patron reserves on it yet, but she didn't like to keep new books off the shelves any longer than she had to—particularly books that circulated as well as mysteries did. This one was fairly fast reading, and she should be able to skim 'through it in an hour or two. If she could concentrate on it, that is.

But she couldn't, she found out in short order. Despite the fact that the phone didn't ring and that even Muldoon settled down on the back of the recliner chair across the room to stare quietly out the window, Val was barely able to make sense out of individual sentences, let alone entire paragraphs or pages. After less than ten minutes, she gave up in disgust at herself.

What she needed was something physical, something that didn't require the least bit of thought. Table tennis would be ideal. It was as fast and strenuous as any sport, and, despite her diminutive size, she was an excellent player. Excellent for Hazleton, that is, though she hadn't rated all that high in Milwaukee. Still, she had found she could safely give Dan at least five points any day of the week, despite his huge advantage in height and reach. Unfortunately, the only place in Hazleton that had a table was Kemper's bowling alley, and it closed at ten.

Finally, swearing to herself, she put a couple Leo Kottke records on and wondered once again how he managed to get some of those sounds out of a guitar. Cranking the volume up so that the sound would carry to the whole house, she hurried to the kitchen and, with a grimace, attacked the sink of dirty dishes. Then, when the dishes succumbed in short order, she started dusting and cleaning the rest of the house. As long as she couldn't concentrate on reading, she might as well try to get caught up on a few of the things she hated to do but couldn't escape for any length of time.

She was getting the vacuum cleaner out of the hall closet next to her bedroom when the phone rang. Glancing at her watch and seeing that it was a couple of minutes after eleven, she knew that it must be her mother, calling from Milwaukee. Eleven was when the long-distance discount rate went up to 60 percent, and eleven-oh-two was when her mother made her occasional calls.

This time her mother's first words were, "How *could* you? I hope you will at *least* invite me to the *wedding!*"

Mildred Carson, Val thought, sighing. Mildred must have seen the announcement in the paper and called Val's mother already, not even waiting for the 60 percent discount. Mildred was a middle-aged—early fifties—woman Val's mother had met during her one visit to Hazleton a couple of weeks after Val moved there. The two women, both widows with grown daughters living hundreds of miles away, hit it off instantly. And, just as a friendly gesture, Mildred had volunteered to keep Val's mother "informed."

When Val explained that Mildred was mistaken, despite what the paper said, her mother seemed both relieved and disappointed. Relieved that her daughter hadn't been holding out on her, but disappointed that the engagement wasn't real.

"I told you you should never have left Milwaukee for that little burg," her mother said resentfully. "You just don't have a decent choice of eligible men."

Shaking her head, Val steered the conversation to other topics before her mother could once again bring up the fact that Millie, Val's younger sister, had been married for more than a year now. The fact that the marriage wasn't working and that Millie was already talking about divorce—talking to Val, at least, if not to their mother—didn't seem to faze her at all. Millie was married, and that was the important thing.

They talked for more than a quarter of an hour. Needless to say, Val didn't tell her mother about the second half of the so-called joke.

The next day was one of Val's nine-to-five shifts at the library instead of the more common noon-to-eight. The weather itself was so crisp and clear, with just a few high clouds bustling across the blue of the sky, that she decided to walk the mile or so to the library. Slipping her new, blue-green poncho on over a dark blouse and slacks, she checked Muldoon's water dish and hurried out the door. Mornings like this always invigorated her, though she was never able to name a reason, and this one was no exception. Even yesterday afternoon's announcement in the *Tribune* and the bizarre note attached to Muldoon's collar were now more a matter of curiosity than concern.

By the time she reached the downtown area, with its three-block, T-shaped business section and turreted courthouse, she had decided that her usual head-on approach to the matter would be the best. That is, she would try to find out who was responsible for the "joke" and, if successful, simply confront him—or her—and ask point-blank what the devil the idea was. She probably wouldn't be able to find out who was behind it, she knew, but on a morning like this, it didn't matter. The attempt was what counted.

She made an abrupt turn from the sidewalk into the *Tribune* office. A half-dozen desks were arranged in an open area behind a high counter. At the rear of the area was a glassed-in cubicle, the editor's office. Katherine Roberts, however, was nowhere to be seen, and Val stood looking around for a familiar face. After a few seconds, a young girl looked up from one of the desks.

"Can I help you? If you want to place a classified ad, the forms are—"

Val shook her head. "I'm looking for the society page editor."

The girl smiled uncertainly. She looked as if she were barely out of high school, her long blond hair and freckles making her look vaguely like a very young Doris Day. "That's me, for the time being," she said. "What can I do for you? I'm Doreen Farr, by the way."

"I'm Valerie Hamilton. I read the—"

"Congratulations on your engagement," the girl said, her face suddenly brightening. She stood up and hurried to the counter, bringing a small notepad with her. "Now if you could just tell me when the wedding is going to be. Normally that sort of thing is included in the announcement of the engagement, but this time—"

"There isn't going to be any wedding," Val said hastily.

"You've broken up already?" The girl's toothy smile faded. "I *am* sorry to hear that. What happened?"

"Nothing happened!" Val said, a little more emphatically than she had intended. "It's just that I was never engaged to Martin Forster—or anyone else—in the first place."

The girl's eyes widened, as if unable to comprehend such a disastrous possibility. "You're sure about that? Absolutely sure?"

"I'm positive."

The girl shook her head, frowning, and a series of muttered expletives escaped her wholesome lips. "You want us to print a retraction, right?" she asked.

"I think that's being taken care of," Val said. "At least Martin said he was going to ask for one. But what I'm interested in is where you got the information in the first place."

"From Mr. Forster, of course," the girl said, a note of indignation in her voice.

Val frowned. Martin? Playing a joke? "When did he tell you about it?"

"Yesterday morning. But I don't understand. If *he* doesn't know whether or not the two of you are engaged—"

"You're positive it was Martin Forster? You recognized him?"

The girl blinked, suddenly uncomfortable. "Well, not exactly. But he *said* he was."

"You don't know Martin by sight, then? Would you recognize the man again?"

"Well . . ."

"You wouldn't recognize him?"

"I only talked to him on the *phone*. And he *said* he was Martin Forster. I didn't see any reason for him to lie to me, you know."

"Did you call him back to check?"

"Call him back? Why should I do that?"

Val sighed. "To verify that it was really Martin Forster who called you in the first place. You know, the way a pizza carry-out store calls back to confirm your order."

The girl shook her head. "I never thought of it. I mean, people call in stories all the time. Why should anyone lie about something like that?"

"That's what I was hoping to find out. I don't suppose you'd recognize the voice if you heard it again?"

The girl shrugged uncertainly. "It was just a voice. A man's voice," she added helpfully.

And that was that, Val thought. "All right. Thanks anyway."

The girl's smile reappeared momentarily but then vanished as she leaned forward over the counter, glancing apprehensively toward the editor's cubicle. "You really *do* want us to print that retraction, then?"

Because of the mile walk and the brief stop at the *Tribune,* Val was a couple of minutes late arriving at the library, a square, blocky building just beyond the downtown area. Sarah Allen, one of the aides, already had the doors unlocked and was settling down behind the check-out desk. She was about the same age as Val's mother, slightly graying and slightly overweight, today in a flowered blouse and pleated skirt. Sarah had been, during Val's first three months, the backbone of the library. She had been there almost as long as Flora Shoemaker, the retiring head librarian, and she knew all the routines, all the foibles of the filing system and card catalogue, and very nearly all the patrons. Without Sarah, Val would've tripped over her own inexperienced feet more often than she liked to think about during the first weeks, but by the second month she had gotten the hang of most things.

"Congratulations!" Sarah said the moment Val pushed through the wide glass doors. "Does this mean we'll be needing another new librarian one of these days?"

Val shook her head as she stopped next to the check-out desk. "I assume you're referring to the thing in yesterday's paper?"

"Of course. I think it's wonderful, you and that nice Mr. Forster."

"In the first place, getting married doesn't mean I'd quit my job. And in the second place, I'm not engaged to anyone, least of all Martin Forster. I barely know the man. The whole thing was someone's idea of a joke."

Sarah's rounded face fell, then took on an angry frown. "Who would want to do a thing like that?"

"I don't know," Val said. "I was just talking to the society editor, and all she knew was that a man phoned the story in yesterday. A man who *said* he was Martin Forster."

The older woman clucked sympathetically. "That's cruel, it really is. I just can't imagine who could be mean enough to do a thing like that to that poor Mr. Forster, after all he's been through."

Val looked at Sarah curiously. "What's he been through?"

Sarah's eyes widened. "You didn't know?"

"Know what? Come on, Sarah, don't you go mysterious on me, too. Martin already did that number last night."

"Then you really don't know? You don't know what happened to his wife?"

"I didn't even know he was ever married. Now what's this all about?"

Sarah leaned forward, glancing toward the door to make sure no patrons were on their way in to interrupt. Then, lowering her voice: "Sandra was killed. Murdered, the poor thing. They'd only been married a week or two, not even through with the honeymoon, I wouldn't imagine."

Suddenly the air seemed to turn cold around Val. She swallowed, trying to get rid of the tightness that gripped her throat. So *that* was why the announcement and the note had upset Martin so much—and why he hadn't told her the real reason. The "joke" was a lot more serious, a lot sicker than she had thought.

If it was a joke.

"How did it happen?" Val asked. "Who killed her?"

"She was strangled, the poor dear, right in her own living

room! Even with all the warnings, they didn't save her! Or even find out who did it!" Sarah shook her head angrily. "It was a disgrace, plain and simple!"

Something grabbed at the pit of Val's stomach. "Warnings?" she asked, wondering if her voice sounded as shaky as she suddenly felt.

Sarah nodded emphatically. "The threats. The poor girl was terrorized for weeks!"

"What kind of threats?" Val asked, though she was sure she already knew the answer.

"Threats on her life! There were letters and calls and—" Sarah broke off, shaking her head at the memory.

"And they never found out who they were from?" Val asked.

"No one ever found out *anything!*" Sarah said indignantly. Then, abruptly, her face softened and lengthened. "That poor Mr. Forster. I hope they find out who's playing this terrible prank."

Val started to ask something else, but she stopped as the front door opened and an elderly couple entered, each carrying two or three books, and approached the check-out desk.

"I'm sure they will," Val said without conviction. Glancing at her watch, she hurried away from the desk, making her way past the card catalogue to her small, cluttered office just off the head of the stairs that led down to the basement. For a moment the stacks of unfiled pamphlets, uncompleted book order forms, and unread book selection material on the bookcase beneath the office's only window leaped out at her, much as the unwashed dishes had the night before, but she knew that these couldn't be disposed of nearly as quickly or as easily. If she didn't make a dent in them today, she would have to start dragging them home, and soon.

Dropping her purse on the bookcase next to the stack of review magazines and hanging her poncho precariously on the one hanger suspended from the coat rack in the corner, she gathered up as much unfinished business as she could and hurried to the reference desk out on the floor of the library, not far from the card catalogue. Mornings were usually the slowest

time of day, so if she were going to get anything accomplished
aside from answering patron questions, she had better get
moving.

She did manage to get most of the book order slips made
out, despite the perpetually balky typewriter, but the bibliogra-
phies—one on utopias and dystopias, one on depression-era
fiction, and one on biographies of explorers—which she had
promised various teachers at the high school were no further
along than they had been twenty-four hours before. At least,
though, she didn't have the "reluctant readers" one to worry
about anymore. After nearly a week's off-and-on work, she had
finished it last Wednesday, and Rena Wright, one of the Eng-
lish teachers, had picked it up Thursday and had already
passed it out to all of her classes and to most of the other
teachers. Whether it would do any good remained to be seen,
although Val had already noticed that at least a half dozen of
the titles on the list were missing from the library's paperback
racks. This meant, she hoped, that they had been checked out
rather than ripped off, though Sarah was generally pretty good
at keeping an eye on the racks, even when she was doing other
things.

Most of this particular day, however, seemed to be a contin-
uation of the evening before, and Val spent an inordinate
amount of time warding off congratulations, best wishes, and
the like. Apparently everyone in Hazleton had seen the society
page the night before or had been told about it by friends.
Every casual acquaintance Val had made in her three months
at the library showed up sometime during the day. The reaction
to her disclaimer varied. Trudy Bowers, the children's librarian,
who had dated Martin a couple of times last year, was obviously not overly upset that he was still eligible, though, with her
short skirts and boots, she hardly seemed Martin's type. Cecil
Willis—a balding, round-faced member of the library board
who apparently equated marriage with children and automatic
retirement—seemed relieved that they would not have to start
an immediate search for yet another librarian. Other reactions
varied from politely regretful through tearfully sorrowful to

righteously indignant that the *Tribune* would print such an un-
founded claim or that someone could be so thoughtless as to
play such a cruel trick on anyone, let alone Martin Forster. By
late morning, Val was seriously considering having a sign taped
to the front door explaining the mistake and perhaps offering a
reward—cancellation of an overdue fine, maybe—to anyone who
could tell her who had called in the phony news item in the first
place.

Then, just before noon, Sheriff Mel Lawrence came in. For-
tyish, slightly overweight with reddish, tightly curling hair, he
wasted no time on preliminaries once they had moved off the
floor and into Val's tiny office.

"You found this attached to your cat's collar last night?" he
asked, holding the note out for Val to see.

She looked at the precise, block capitals and nodded. "It
looks like the same one. Martin gave it to you?"

"That's right. Now, did you actually find it yourself? Or was
it Forster?"

She frowned up at him as he returned the note to his already
crowded shirt pocket opposite his badge. "I suppose you could
say we both found it."

"How so?"

"Martin saw there was something on Muldoon's collar, but I
was the one who took it off the collar. Why?"

"Could you tell me exactly what happened?"

"I could. But didn't Martin tell you all this?"

"He did. But I'd like to hear it from you, if you don't mind."

She stared at him a moment, irritated, but then she shrugged.
"All right, if that's what you want." In a few sentences, she
outlined Muldoon's return to the house and the discovery of the
note. "And in case you're trying to keep me in the dark," she
finished, "don't bother. I already know what happened to Martin's wife. Sarah told me."

A slight frown wrinkled his brow as he glanced toward the
door of the office. "How much did she tell you?"

"Her name was Sandra, she was murdered, and she was terrorized by a number of 'warnings.' What were the warnings, by the way? Notes like that one?"

He hesitated, then nodded as he seemed to reach a decision. "Partly. The first one was a note identical to this one in every way. It was even wrapped around a cat's collar, just like this one."

"Oh? No wonder Martin was so upset. But what else was there? What do I have to look forward to if this joker keeps going?"

"You think it's a joke, then?"

"What else could it be? Between that note and the engagement announcement—you did see the announcement, didn't you?"

"Forster pointed it out to me when he brought the note in."

"Well? What else could it be but a joke?"

"You're probably right. That's what Forster thinks, at least."

"And you?"

He shrugged. "As you said, what else could it be? There's certainly no one in Hazleton with a reason to kill you. Is there?"

"Not that I know of. But you still haven't answered my question. If this so-called joke continues, what do I have to look forward to?"

"Phone calls, a lot of them. Mrs. Forster got a dozen or more over a three-week period."

"No more notes?"

"Just one, the night before she was killed." He hesitated, his eyes avoiding hers for a moment. "It was attached to her cat's collar, like the first one."

"She couldn't recognize the voice on the phone? Or have the calls traced?"

Lawrence shook his head. "It was only a whisper. And by the time we arranged to have her calls traced, it was too late."

"She couldn't tell anything from what the caller said? No hints as to who it might have been?"

"When you phone someone you're planning to kill, you don't

leave your name and number. Look, Miss Hamilton, are you sure you want to go into all this?"

"Of course!" she snapped, irritated at his condescending tone. "Martin may be the primary target of the joke, but if last night is any indication, it looks as if I'm directly in the line of fire. I think I'm at least entitled to know what's going on."

He looked at her somberly for a moment, and then shrugged. "I suppose you do, at that. But there isn't that much to know."

"But if he talked to Mrs. Forster that many times, he must've said *something*."

"Oh, yes, he said plenty. And everything he said pointed to ex-boyfriends. The only trouble was, half of Hazleton qualified as ex-boyfriends. And each call either pointed to a different one or to none at all."

"For instance?"

"It's been five years!" Lawrence said in sudden irritation. "I can't remember every little detail!"

"But certainly one or two of the—"

"I'm sorry, no, not a one! And I didn't come here to stand around wracking my brain trying to remember!"

"Then why did you come?"

"I came because of the note," he said, lowering his voice and pulling in a deep breath to calm himself. "I wanted to ask you if you had any idea who might have sent it. Do you?"

"None. Except that he—or she—knows my cat. And either has a very strong grudge against Martin or has a very sick sense of humor. Or both."

Lawrence nodded. "I'd also like you to promise me something."

"What?" She frowned suspiciously.

"That you'll call me the instant anything else happens—*if* anything does."

"The phone calls, you mean?"

"Anything. Anything at all."

His tone, suddenly businesslike and deadly serious, sent a twinge through her stomach. "You certainly don't think this could be the same person who killed Martin's wife, do you?"

"I doubt it. But anything's possible."

"All right. But I hope you're keeping an eye on Martin. After all, he's the target of all this, not me."

"Don't worry. I told Forster the same thing. And don't forget," he said, turning to go, "anytime, anywhere. Someone at the office always knows how to reach me."

She watched as he made his way through the library, pausing only to nod to Sarah Allen at the check-out desk. She felt, she had to admit, just a little more uneasy than she had before.

The problem of the note and her uneasiness, however, was pushed out of her mind entirely a few minutes later. Edna Plover arrived.

As usual, the woman swept in through the wide, plate-glass doors, casting haughtily disapproving glances at almost everything, but particularly at the racks of dog-eared paperbacks and at Trudy Bowers' knee-length boots and slightly shorter than necessary skirt. Normally, Mrs. Plover would pause to inspect the display of recently acquired books next to the check-out desk, but this time she veered past them without a glance and headed straight for Val's desk. A tall, graying woman in her early sixties, Mrs. Plover would have cut an impressive figure if it weren't for the hat, a slant-brimmed, flowered creation with a short veil. In Val's eyes, at least, it totally wiped out the effect of the obviously expensive autumn-rust dress and half-length brown fur jacket she wore. For whatever reason, most of Edna Plover's hats—and she had one for every occasion—reminded Val of a highbrow Minnie Pearl.

Val sighed silently as the woman approached. Edna Plover was Martin Forster's aunt, but that was incidental except insofar as it was evidence that stuffiness as well as height and slenderness was hereditary. What concerned Val was the woman's role as a hyperactive representative of the "Decent Literature" movement that was, unfortunately, becoming more and more vocal around the country. Flora Shoemaker, the retiring head librarian, had warned Val about her, but Edna Plover had to be seen and heard to be fully appreciated.

"Some organizations of that type are almost reasonable,"

Flora had said, "but not Edna and her chums. You can take it for granted that *nothing*—nothing short of putting Edna in charge of selecting all books the library buys, that is—will make them happy. And that's to your advantage in a way. They're *so* far out they don't have a lot of support, even here. But they do have some, and they do make a lot of noise, so be careful. And don't forget, in the Hazleton Public Library, you don't have the bureaucracy to protect you the way you have in Milwaukee or any large system."

Val had laughed. "I'll take my chances on Edna. The bureaucracy may protect you, but that's not all it does, believe me."

"Can I help you?" Val asked as Mrs. Plover came to a halt in front of her desk. The smile on Val's face was forced but polite.

Mrs. Plover held out one gloved hand and dropped a half-dozen sheets of paper onto the already cluttered desk next to the ancient typewriter. "You have, I think, helped quite enough, thank you," she said, her voice even tighter and more clipped than usual.

Val looked down at the papers and suppressed a groan as she recognized them—her "reluctant readers" bibliography. She had expected a reaction, but not quite this soon.

"Yes," Val said, picking up the list and glancing at it, "I was rather happy with this myself." She gestured toward the paperback racks. "I think it's already had a few results. A number of the books on the list have been checked out recently."

Mrs. Plover snatched the list from Val's hand, all but waving it in her face. "May I ask precisely what purpose you think is served by this collection of trash?"

"This listing of books, you mean?" Val asked, managing to keep her voice pleasant.

"If you care to honor them with the term 'books,' yes. Obviously your definition of the word is a good deal broader than mine."

"I see. Would you care to see some of the titles on the list? Most of them are on the shelves."

"I most certainly would *not!*"

"You're already familiar with the titles, then?"

"I am as familiar as I care to be, and I have no intention of becoming any *more* familiar with such rubbish!"

Val shrugged almost imperceptibly. "As you wish. Then how *can* I be of service?"

Mrs. Plover's gray eyes seemed to flash below the short veil. "You can enlighten me as to the meaning of this—this list. The daughter of a close friend of mine brought it home from school, just this noon. I was given to understand that she—and her entire class!—received it from a *teacher.*"

Val nodded. "That's no doubt correct. Mrs. Wright picked up the original list late last week. I understand she planned to distribute copies to her classes and to see if other teachers were interested in doing the same."

"But why—"

"As I recall, Mrs. Wright requested it." Val put on her most disarming smile, though she knew it was wasted, as was her explanation. "You are no doubt aware of the trend away from reading. Well, some of the teachers at the high school are trying to reverse that trend, at least in their own classes. This bibliography simply lists a number of books that we thought might lure a few of the kids away from television for a few hours now and then."

"Then you *are* admitting that you devised this list? That this is, in effect, your perverted version of a list of recommended books?"

"If you care to call it that, yes. Oh, I'm sure there are more literarily acceptable books available, but—"

"I am quite sure of that as well!" Mrs. Plover snapped. "*I* could give you a list—a worthwhile list!"

"I'm sure you could, but you have to understand—this list is aimed at children who otherwise wouldn't read at all. The idea is—"

"The idea *is,* it seems obvious to me, to foist your own perverted standards even onto our educational system! And may I say that this time you have overstepped yourself! Even Mrs. Shoemaker never went *this* far!"

"I'm sorry you feel that way," Val said, refusing to raise her voice, "but I don't really know what could be done at this point."

For a long moment Mrs. Plover stood stiffly in front of Val's desk. Then, abruptly, she seemed to calm herself, a faint, lofty smile appearing on her narrow, angular face—a face, Val noted absently, that did bear a certain structural resemblance to that of her nephew, Martin Forster.

"I don't believe you have ever attended one of our meetings, Ms. Hamilton," Mrs. Plover said, her voice now soft and sugar coated except for the faintly disapproving emphasis on the "Ms."

"No," Val admitted, "I just haven't had a lot of time, I'm afraid. But you can be sure I'm aware of your group."

"I'm sure you are. But I feel, very strongly, that you should *make* the time. I'm sure that, if you could meet the other members of our group, if you could hear their opinions and views, you would gain a better insight into our goals. It could be of some importance, particularly in light of the fact that the library board is meeting next week, and that the public is invited to be heard at that meeting."

A threat? Val wondered. Then, mentally, she sighed. She had known, from Flora Shoemaker's first warning about the group, that she would eventually have to go to one of their meetings, so she might as well get it over with. There was, after all, an old saying about there being an advantage in knowing your enemy.

"Perhaps you're right," Val said. "I must admit, I have been curious."

Mrs. Plover's faint smile took on a touch of smugness at Val's capitulation. Even her voice reflected a certain self-satisfaction as she told Val when and where her group's next meeting—dinner at Arlen's, one of the more expensive restaurants in the Hazleton area—would be. "You will be our guest, of course," she finished graciously as she turned and, not even bothering to give another disapproving glance at either Trudy or the paperback racks, swept out.

Chapter 3

Val left the library a little before six, leaving Trudy Bowers and one of the part-time aides, Angie Harris, in charge. Muldoon, of course, was sonaring up a storm as Val let herself in, so cat food was the first order of business. She thought about a snack for herself, but realized she didn't feel like it. In fact, she probably wouldn't want much of anything this evening at all, not until her "performance" was over. She was used to singing at parties or picnics, where things were more informal and there were other singers and guitars to trade off with—and where it was strictly for fun. But this, where there would be relative strangers, and where money was to be raised . . .

She shook her head, trying to remember whose idea the fund raiser had been, but she couldn't pin it down. Like Topsy, it seemed to have just grown, though she did remember that Katherine Roberts had certainly been one of the early boosters and had given the event as much publicity in the *Tribune* as she could. It had gotten started at one of the "welcome the new librarian" parties that Katherine, as president of the library board, had given. Someone—probably Val herself—had remarked on the lack of cassette tapes at the library, and everyone had agreed it was a shame but there just wasn't enough money in the budget to buy any. Someone else had suggested a benefit or some kind of fund-raising party, and it had built from there. Everyone, including Val, had had one or two drinks, and by the time the evening was over, a brand new organization—Friends of the Hazleton Library, Cassette Division—had been formed. And Val, half jokingly, had agreed to bring her guitar to the event if someone else brought a tambourine. The next day, when the mild euphoria of the drinks had worn off, the idea didn't seem nearly as good as it had the night before, but like most things, once it was started, it was impossible to stop. Katherine had even bought a tambourine especially for the occasion, though she refused to say who was going to play it. Someone else reserved a room at the Civic Center.

And now that it was upon her, Val had to admit that she had something akin to opening-night jitters. In fact, as the time drew nearer, she began to realize that, in a strange way, she was grateful for the phony engagement announcement with its attendant confusion, even grateful for the irascible Plover's brief appearance. Such distractions had kept her mind occupied, and she hadn't, until now, been given much time to worry, which had kept the stage-fright butterflies to a minimum.

They were at a maximum, however, when Dan Richards arrived at her door a little after six-thirty. As always, he was tieless, his off-blond hair falling over his forehead and curling around his ears and over the collar of his dark blue, almost black knit shirt.

He looked down at her for a second, his blue and always-animated eyes taking in her uncharacteristically solemn face and briskly nervous movements as she motioned him inside.

"If you don't mind my saying so," he said, "you look just a smidge uptight."

"Congratulations on your uncanny perception. But you look relaxed enough for both of us."

He shrugged loosely. "I try. It isn't easy, though, being both a lawyer and a relaxed human being. Anything I can do to help?"

She shook her head. "I doubt it, not right now."

"How about a good meal? Would that help settle you down? We had planned to have dinner before this evening's entertainment, you may remember."

"I remember, but I don't feel like much of anything right now. Maybe afterward. Right now, the butterflies don't leave a lot of room for food."

"Whatever you want," he said, picking up her guitar case

from where it was leaning against the end of the couch. "You're the star tonight."

Val laughed, more than a little nervously. "Thanks a lot. You're not helping matters."

"Don't worry, it'll be fine. Everyone's on your side."

"I know, I know. Everyone but me and the butterflies."

Dan looked at her thoughtfully for a second, then abruptly turned to the door. "Come on," he said, "I've got something to show you."

Without waiting for a reply, he pushed through the door and loped across the lawn to his two-tone red Checker and dumped the guitar into the foyer-sized back seat as he slid behind the wheel. Leaning across the seat, he unlatched the passenger's-side door and let it swing open. By the time Val reached the car and got in, he had the huge glove compartment open and was extracting a small cassette recorder. As she slammed the door, he pushed one of the controls briefly, then laid the recorder on top of the dash and pressed the "Play" button.

A husky contralto issued from the tiny speaker. Though she couldn't place the voice, the words were all too familiar—the last few lines of "The Vicar of Bray." Automatically, the words formed lightly on her own lips even as she looked puzzledly at Dan. " 'For in my faith and loyalty, I never more will falter, And George my lawful king shall be, Until the times do alter.' "

Then the voice fell silent, and Dan snapped off the player.

"Pretty good, right?" he asked, grinning.

"Pretty good, yes. But who is it?"

"You don't recognize the voice? You obviously recognized the song."

She shook her head. "But I think I'd like to meet her."

His grin broadened. He held the cassette flat in the palm of his hand, like a waiter serving dinner. Looking from the cassette to Val and back, he said, in mock formal tones, "Valerie Hamilton, meet Valerie Hamilton."

"What? What the devil are you talking about?"

Instead of saying anything, he rewound the tape briefly and again punched the "Play" button. As it finished a second time, he said, still grinning, "Didn't realize you sounded that good, did you?"

"That's *me?* Where did you get it?"

"You don't remember singing that song, oh, in the past three or four weeks?"

She started to shake her head, but then she looked at him, frowning. "Just at that party at your place. Don't tell me—"

She stopped as she saw him making a "you got it" sign with his thumb and forefinger. "How did you do it?"

"It's a small recorder," he said. "And when you start singing, you're not totally in touch with your environment anymore."

"What you're saying is, I don't pay attention to what's going on around me?"

"If you want to put it that crudely, yes. And your eyes do tend to glaze over just a bit when you really get going. But from your reaction, I take it you've never listened to yourself before?"

She shook her head. "Never. Not singing, anyway. Listening to a tape of me just talking makes me nervous enough, which was something that drove me up the wall in speech classes in college. Incidentally, I thought bugging people without a court order was illegal. Is that any way for a lawyer to act?"

He shrugged. "Lawyers are people, too. Most of them, at least. But now that you've heard how great you sound, you're glad I did it, right?"

"I don't know. Now that I think back, it didn't sound all that great. Look, how much did you record?"

"About twenty minutes. Mostly pretty good stuff. And I was hoping to get enough more to fill out the tape tonight."

"Now wait just a minute! I didn't say—"

"It's for a good cause. What I plan to do, see, is donate the tape to the library. A seed, so to speak, around which the cassette collection can grow. You can't be so un-civic-minded that you'd refuse." Before she could say anything in further protest, he tossed the recorder into the back seat next to his rust blazer.

"And now that that's all settled," he said, starting the car, "are you still refusing to eat?"

In the end they got some tacos—one for her, three for him—at the new drive-in at the south end of town by the railroad tracks. Then, with almost an hour to survive and a herd of butterflies still to subdue, they went to Kemper's bowling alley to see if Hazleton's only public Ping-Pong table was available. It was, and in the next forty minutes Val managed to win only a little over half their games, despite the fact that she spotted Dan only four points a game instead of the usual five or six.

The exercise, though it successfully battered Val's butterflies into temporary submission, necessitated a quick trip back to her house to change into a fresh sweater. When she asked Dan if he didn't need a fresh shirt himself—"You weren't exactly standing still, even if you did lose"—he shook his head.

"Don't worry about it," he said, keeping a more or less straight face. "I'll put my jacket on, and I just won't let anyone sniff my armpits this evening."

Despite the delay, they reached the Civic Center—formerly Hazleton High School—only a minute or two after eight. Their footsteps echoed from the bare walls and high ceilings as they hurried along the first-floor hallway to the meeting room, the former assembly hall, from which all the bolted down seats and desks had been removed to make room for varying numbers of folding chairs.

Glancing around as they entered, Val was relieved to see that Katherine and the rest of the Cassette Committee had cleared the chairs out of the room, leaving only a table at one end, which they had covered with a dozen different kinds of snacks and soft drinks. The atmosphere was much closer to that of a party than a performance, and there were several slacks and sweaters not unlike her own, even a few jeans, and only one or two ties among the men. Even so, the butterflies staged a minor comeback as Katherine Roberts, her square, almost mannish face softened by a wide smile, got everyone's attention and gave Val an introduction, and asked for requests. The party atmosphere reasserted itself, though, when Dan made the first request, for "Flora, the Lily of the West," in honor of Flora Shoemaker, Val's Fay-Bainterlike predecessor at the library. After a couple of lines, he even joined in himself with a lively if uneven baritone.

And so it went. Trudy Bowers, complete with an even shorter skirt than she had worn at the library that day, showed up a few minutes later and promptly revealed that she was Katherine's "mystery tambourinest." Then, while Dan and Val led the audience in the proper sequence of cheers and boos, Trudy belted out something she called "The Salvation Army Song," the ending of which—"All I do is stand here and beat this blank-blank drum!"—made Val wish she had managed to learn "Sam Hall" after all. It would have fit the mood perfectly.

In short, Val forgot all about her butterflies and didn't think about the threatening note even once, and before the evening was over, the thirty-odd people who attended had come up with close to four hundred dollars, including one anonymous envelope with fifty dollars inside.

When things started breaking up around ten-thirty, Val noticed Martin and wondered when he had arrived. She was sure he hadn't been there at the start. His somber face and vested conservatism would have been very noticeable. As he approached her from one direction, Dan appeared from the other, his cassette recorder in one hand.

"A little cavernous sounding," Dan said, "but not bad, considering it was recorded in a cavern. Would you care to hear a snatch?"

"Only if you had the guts to record your own bellowing," she said, laughing despite the fact that the thought of the tape—forgotten until now—still made her oddly nervous.

"But of course. And your leggy friend's tambourine bashing as well. Who knows, this could be the start of a whole new career for you."

She shook her head. "No, thanks. I'd just as soon keep it a hobby—and fun, not work."

Dan shrugged. "And here I was going to offer to be your manager." He noticed Martin then. "What about you, sir? As an unbiased observer and momentary fiancé, don't you think she could carve a niche for herself in the world of professional vocalists?"

"You were very good," Martin said, ignoring Dan's banter. As he looked down at Val, she noticed there were beads of perspiration on his forehead, and the room was not all that warm. "Can I speak with you for a minute?"

When Val hesitated, Dan shrugged again. "Why not? After all, you were engaged to her for almost a whole day, which is better than I've been able to do." He glanced toward the table, where some of the snacks still remained. "I'll be over there, fighting off starvation."

As Dan moved away, Martin took Val's arm and, stiffly, urged her out of the room and into the barren, echoing hallway.

"Did the sheriff speak to you today?" he asked as they moved a few feet away from the door.

She nodded and recounted Lawrence's visit, including his admonition to call him if anything at all out of the ordinary happened. As she finished, she shook her head, frowning. "But I got the distinct feeling that he wasn't telling me everything."

"Possibly not. But it would be best if you did exactly as he wishes."

"You sound as if *you're* taking it a little more seriously than you were last night." She put a hand on his arm. "You haven't changed your mind about its being just a bad joke, have you?"

He shook his head sharply. "No, nothing like that. Nothing like that at all. It's just . . ." His voice trailed off as he nervously moistened his lips. "It's just that I've been thinking about it ever since. I can't *help* thinking about it. I know that I'm the one it's aimed at, but there *is* something you have to know." He brushed at his forehead, nervously wiping away the perspiration.

"Whatever it is," she said, "you don't have to tell me. Just because some cretin out there has decided to—"

"No!" he said, his voice suddenly harsh, though barely above a whisper. "I *do* have to tell you! You could be in danger!"

"Me in danger? But why? Even on the remote chance that

these things aren't strictly a joke, I wouldn't be in any danger unless I married you. And the retraction should have taken care of that."

"I don't understand it either," he said, and his eyes darted briefly around the high-ceilinged, dimly lit corridor as another couple emerged from the assembly hall and walked echoingly toward the huge doors at the far end. He looked back at her. "All I know is, whoever killed Sandra was never apprehended. You knew that, didn't you? Lawrence did tell you that no one was ever even arrested?"

"He told me. But you're certainly not trying to tell me that this same person might be the one who sent the note—are you? Or that he might actually try to kill me? It doesn't make sense."

"I know it doesn't. And if it were anyone but you, I wouldn't even bring the subject up."

She frowned. "Me? What's so special about me?"

He stood motionless, and then slowly reached into his jacket pocket and brought out his wallet. "Have you ever seen a picture of Sandra?" he asked.

"Of course not. But what does that have to do with anything?" Lord, she thought apprehensively, I hope he's not going to go maudlin on me.

"Here," he said, pulling a small black-and-white snapshot from one of the pockets of the wallet and handing it to her.

"Sandra?" she asked, taking the picture gingerly.

"Yes," he said, "it's Sandra. Does she look familiar to you?"

Val held the picture so as to get the best illumination from the bare bulb high in the ceiling. The smiling face was slender but the lips were full. The eyes, though deepset, seemed to sparkle. The hair, cut almost as short as Val's own, was dark and curly.

"Sorry," she said, and for an instant a morbid image of the woman's face staring blindly out of a coffin darted through Val's mind. "She was very pretty," Val said, uneasily conscious of the past tense of the verb, "but she doesn't look familiar. Should she?"

"She doesn't remind you of anyone?"

Val shook her head as she handed the picture back. Martin held it in the dim light for a moment, then looked down at Val. His eyes moved slowly, uneasily, over her face, as if searching for something he didn't really want to find.

"Try looking in a mirror," he said softly.

Dan held his curiosity in check all through the late supper at the Streamliner—the "good" restaurants had all closed by that time—and didn't question Val as they drove, windows rolled up against the damp night air, the two miles around the edge of Hazleton to Val's house near the northwest city limits.

Switching off the Checker, he turned toward her on the high, bench-style seat. The light from a streetlamp a dozen yards away—the only one in this half of the block—shone dimly through the windshield, hitting his face at an angle that made the small scar on the corner of his jaw, normally barely visible, stand out in relief.

"Obviously," he said, "since you haven't yet told me what Marty's urgent business this evening was, you are going to invite me in so you can explain. Correct?"

"Of course," she said, manufacturing a hasty smile. She reached into the back seat for the guitar case but missed it as Dan snatched it up and slid out of the car with it. Pausing to dig her keys from her purse, she followed him.

"Something serious, was it?" he asked as he waited for her to unlock the front door.

"I don't know," she said, pushing the door open and gesturing for him to put the guitar case in the corner of the living room between the couch and the bookcase on which her stereo sat. "Maybe you can tell me."

"Glad to render an opinion, if I have one."

There was a thump of padded feet hitting the floor somewhere down the hall, and Muldoon sonared into the living room and looked around curiously. Dan leaned down and snatched the cat up, cradling him on his back in the crook of one arm, lightly scratching his shaggy stomach with the other hand. As the cat began to purr lightly and flex his claws in the air, Dan lowered himself onto one end of the couch.

"Well?" he prompted. "You were about to unburden yourself about Marty."

Nodding, she dropped onto the couch a few inches from Dan and, kicking off her shoes, tucked her feet underneath herself and leaned back.

Briefly, she told him about the note and the cautions she had gotten from both Martin and the sheriff. His eyes widened as she mentioned the note. He said nothing, but the hand scratching Muldoon's stomach slowed and stopped. When she finished, she looked directly at Dan. "Well? What do *you* think? I might as well get a full range of opinions."

"Whether or not you look like Marty's wife, you mean?" He shrugged, and she wondered if the lightness of the motion was real or was put on for her benefit. "Now that it's been pointed out to me, you do remind me of her a little. But it's only physical, believe me, only physical."

"Oh?" She looked at him questioningly. "Did you know her very well?"

For a time he didn't reply, occupying himself with turning Muldoon right side up and then untangling the cat's claws from the sleeve of his jacket as he set him on the floor.

"Well?" Val asked, ignoring Muldoon as he trotted in the general direction of the kitchen, stopping occasionally to look back over his shoulder hopefully.

"I knew her," he said finally, "but I wouldn't say I knew her very well."

"Now don't *you* start going mysterious on me. You're not the type. Besides, Martin's already done that number."

Abruptly he grinned. "You're right. Okay, a full confession. I knew her. I dated her a couple of times. And I was one of the suspects. Along with Martin and everyone else who ever dated her."

"But you didn't kill her?"

"Hardly. Though I have to admit, as far as the evidence goes, there's nothing to prove that I didn't. No alibi whatsoever. Home alone, no witnesses." He shrugged. "Luckily, very few of the other suspects had alibis either. Except for Marty, of course. He's about the only one with an airtight alibi."

"That's more like it. Now, what did you mean about my resemblance, such as it is, being 'only physical'?"

He hesitated, his face growing serious. "Off the record, okay? Particularly off Marty's record."

"If you say so. But why?"

"Because Marty thought—still thinks—she was perfect, at least after she met him, and he'd not be the easiest person to work in the same office with if he knew what I really thought."

"Okay, I promise. So, what do you really think?"

"That she sold Marty a bill of goods."

"How so?"

"She was—or at least I *think* she was—an opportunist. I don't think she loved—or even particularly liked—Marty when they were married."

"Then why would she marry him?"

"One of the standard reasons. He was a good catch. An up-and-coming young lawyer, headed for good money."

"Sounds like a pretty sexist opinion, if you ask me."

He shook his head, grinning slightly. "Not really. If I had said 'all women,' or even 'most women,' marry for money, *that* would be sexist. I'm just talking about one particular woman. About whom you asked my opinion, by the way."

"Sorry. Keep going. All I know about her so far is that she looked a little like me, she went out with lots of men, and she may have married Martin for his future earning power. What did you mean by her 'selling him a bill of goods'?"

"Simple. As you're no doubt aware, Marty is something of a stuffed shirt."

She shrugged but didn't disagree.

"Anyway," Dan went on, "Sandra was definitely not his type. She played the field, widely and deeply. A new man every few weeks, often overlapping."

"More your type?"

"Somewhat, I suppose, in my reckless youth. More mine

than Marty's, certainly. To oversimplify, she liked one-night stands; Marty wanted a lifetime commitment—after due deliberation—or nothing."

"One-night stands?" Val couldn't help but grin. "You're saying that Sandra was Hazleton's 'loose woman'?"

"They still have them in small towns, believe it or not. Anyway, whatever you call it, that's what she was—until she met Marty. Then she did a total about face. Got religion, so to speak."

"A born-again virgin?"

Dan's eyebrows went up for an instant before he laughed. "Something like that, yes."

"You're sure this wasn't just sour grapes on your part?"

His face turned serious, almost somber, and he shook his head. "I don't think so, but I honest-to-God don't know. I hadn't seen her for several months at that point, but who knows what sort of tricks a jealous subconscious can play?"

"What was supposed to have caused her sudden conversion?"

He shrugged. "I don't know. Marty seemed to think *he* was responsible. Which, in a way, he may have been, if my theory—"

A sudden clatter, as if someone had dropped a metal can half full of buckshot, cut his words short and sent a stiffening jolt through his entire body. His eyes darted around the room, and he felt his heart suddenly pounding.

Then, after a moment's tension-filled silence, Val laughed. "It's just—" she began, then stopped. "Come on, I'll show you."

Taking his hand, she led him quickly down the hall to the kitchen, where she snapped on the light. "It's only Muldoon," she said, still laughing and pointing to where the cat sat on the floor in front of the counter, clawing at the plastic lid on the can of crunchies he had just knocked to the floor.

It was working.

At last the seed was taking root and beginning to grow. Her face—recognizable instantly to anyone but an ostrich like Forster—had at last inched its way through the seemingly endless layers of cowardice and self-imposed blindness, and he had been forced to see it for what it was.

Yes, it was working. There was a long way yet to go, but it was working!

And it was time to begin the next stage, to approach the other principal in the affair.

Sandra's voice, thin and ghostly, filled the air as he dialed, resting the receiver lightly against his ear.

After a half-dozen uncounted rings, a male voice, fogged with sleep, came on the line. "Hello?"

He remained silent, letting the crystalline tones of Sandra's voice float over the wire.

"Who is this?" The voice was suddenly harsh and edged with fear. He continued to listen, silently imagining the thoughts that must be invading the other's mind.

The voice swore, but the line remained open. The fear was obvious in every syllable, in every breath and every pause.

"I said, who is this? What do you want?"

Still he remained silent, waiting, listening, imagining—willing his thoughts through the wires and into the other's mind. Sandra's voice, gathering strength as the song neared its end, continued to flow around him, sweeping across the distance to that other, now silent listener.

Then, suddenly, her voice soared as the final notes passed her long-dead lips, and there was silence.

Into that silence, he spoke, "I know that you murdered her. I have always known, but I have done nothing—until now. Now, at last, the waiting is over. Now you will pay."

Not waiting for a reply, he replaced the receiver in the cradle.

He smiled, seeing the other's fear-wracked face in his mind. It was only a matter of time . . .

Chapter 4

When there were no more mysterious notes and no threatening phone calls during the next couple of days, Val began to relax. It had been a one-shot joke, and it was apparently over. The slight twinges of apprehension mixed with curiosity that surfaced whenever the phone rang or an unfamiliar face appeared began to fade. By Thursday, the evening of the irascible Plover's meeting, she was almost totally back to normal.

Warding off a last-minute offer by Dan to accompany her and provide free legal counsel for the duration of the meal, Val put on her most conservative clothes—pinkish, satiny blouse and sedate skirt and a slightly masculine-looking knit jacket—dabbed on a minuscule amount of perfume, and hurried to her car. As she inserted the key into the ignition, she hesitated, wrinkling her nose as she sniffed the air in the enclosed car curiously. It took her a moment to realize that what she was smelling—a faintly lilac odor, pleasant but a little pungent—was the perfume she had put on. She didn't remember it smelling that way the last time she had used it, but that had been so long ago, she decided quickly, she probably just didn't remember the scent properly. Or perhaps the perfume itself had changed. Like most of her perfumes, she had had it for three or four years, ever since the summer one of the aides in the Milwaukee branch she had worked in had turned part-time Avon lady.

It took only a few minutes to cover the five miles to Arlen's, on the northeast shore of Wilson Lake, west of Hazleton. She parked in the huge lot the restaurant shared with the private golf course across the road. There were a dozen cars, all vastly more expensive than Val's four-year-old Gremlin, but the shrub-lined lot still looked almost deserted. Through a break in the hedges, she could see the lake itself, over a mile wide at this point. The sun, poking through a hole in the clouds near the horizon, glinted redly off the still water.

Bracing herself, Val made her way between the two imitation gaslight streetlamps that acted as gateposts and climbed the rustically rough-hewn steps to the equally rustic and rough-hewn front door. Inside, a hostess guided her through the main dining room to one of the half-dozen meeting rooms in the rear, where she was greeted with restrained enthusiasm by Edna Plover.

The meeting went about as advertised. During the dinner itself—a spicily exotic variety of chicken that was excellent, Val had to admit—Mrs. Plover chatted graciously about the decaying moral state of the country in general and the literary world in particular. Following that, Val was introduced briefly from the speaker's table, following which an out-of-town speaker named Tucker echoed most of the group's philosophy and, at the end, got in a plug for the John Birch Society.

After the formal program, the group milled around in an orderly fashion, most of them expressing personal appreciation to the speaker and then, with abrupt casualness, getting in a word or two with Val. Most of the words, of course, centered on the responsibility of teachers and librarians to be "leaders of community thought, not mere followers." They all acknowledged that the pressures must be tremendous to "go along with the popular whims," but they felt strongly that such pressures must be resisted at all costs. Only twice was the bibliography mentioned directly, and then only as an example of the lengths to which one could be driven if one were not able to resist the "negative pressures of popular taste" that were so often and so blatantly exerted these days. They were all terribly understanding and sympathetic, but there was always the unspoken hint that unless such pressures were more successfully resisted in the future, there were a number of more positive pressures waiting in the wings to be applied. Mrs. Plover, her wine-red dress and ubiquitous half-veiled hat contrasting sharply with the predominantly dark blue and gray crowd, stayed close by

Val at all times. Hardly anyone, Val noticed, spoke to Edna Plover without complimenting her on her outfit, and she took it all as her due, returning the compliments only occasionally and with great restraint.

Finally, as the last of the group paid their respects, Val thanked Mrs. Plover for an "informative evening" and made her escape. As she emerged from the air-conditioned chill of the restaurant into the slightly muggy, late September air, she let her breath out in a whoosh of relief and allowed the neutral smile, which she had somehow maintained through it all, to fade. She stood at the bottom of the steps for several seconds, simply enjoying the air and the sudden feeling of freedom that swept over her. She couldn't remember when she had last had such a "closed-in" feeling. There was something about Plover's group—or perhaps about the way Edna Plover controlled it— that would have given Val claustrophobia even if the meeting had been held in an open field. She should have, she supposed, taken Dan up on his offer of company and counsel. He would at least have livened things up a bit, though she doubted that he would have done much for her relations with the irascible Plover.

Pulling in her breath, she hurried down the steps and across the parking lot to her car. Most of the same dozen cars were still in the lot. Plover's group, she supposed. Three or four others were scattered around, mostly the same expensive varieties. None, she noticed, grinning, had parked anywhere near her own.

Tossing her purse—her miniature, necessities-only model— onto the passenger's seat, Val climbed in and nursed the car to life. On the second try, it caught, and she thought once again that, one of these days before cold weather, she was going to have to get it tuned up. She really should check with Dan or someone at the library and see what garage, if any, could be trusted to do a good job. If Hazleton was like most other places, big and small alike, you had about a fifty-fifty chance of being ripped off one way or another.

Once on the road, she lowered the window a few inches, letting the wind cool her face and tangle her hair. As the narrow blacktop wound its way along the cottages that lined the lake side of the road sporadically, she realized that a faint ache had begun to pull at the base of her skull. She rubbed at it with one hand, pressing against the muscle in the back of her neck, and the pain receded. Just a leftover from Plover's group and all the forced smiling, she told herself.

The lake shore, curving back to the west, retreated from the road, which continued generally south through a wooded area. Here there were no cottages or houses of any kind. The only light, aside from the headlights' beams skidding along the road ahead of her, was the dull skyglow that she knew came from the lights of Hazleton to the east.

As she slowed for a particularly sharp curve and then tried to accelerate, the car hesitated uncertainly before lurching forward again.

Stiffening, Val swore under her breath. What now? Had she waited too long to get the engine tuned up? Her eyes darted to the yellowing blobs that were the dash lights. Plenty of gas, she was relieved to see, and none of the warning lights were on. And the temperature gauge showed on the low side of the normal reading.

She pressed a little harder on the accelerator, and the car responded unsteadily. The speedometer crept up a couple of miles per hour.

Again she cursed silently. Well, as long as it didn't conk out entirely, she was all right. The highway should be around the next curve, and from there it was only about three miles to town. Certainly it would hold together that long.

Cautiously, as the stop sign for the highway appeared dimly in the headlights, she began to slow. She kept one foot on the accelerator, the other on the brake, keeping the engine almost racing as she slowed the car. It was a trick she had learned when her previous car, a badly rusting Chevy, had taken to stalling. She had nursed it halfway across Milwaukee that way once, in an effort to get it repaired on the 30-day warranty the used car dealer had given her.

The woods came to an end just short of the stop sign, giving her a fairly clear view of the highway. She didn't stop completely, only slowed to a little less than ten miles per hour.

Seeing that the highway was clear of approaching headlights for at least a couple of hundred yards in each direction, she pressed down on the gas.

With a lurching cough, the engine fell silent. The "oil" and "generator" lights glowed bright red, and the headlights dimmed noticeably.

Swearing, not quite silently this time, she braked to a sudden stop a dozen yards short of the highway. Hastily, she switched the headlights off and shifted to "park." She twisted the key and pressed down lightly on the gas.

Almost, but not quite.

She tried again. This time it didn't even come close to catching, just a spasmodic cough or two.

And she smelled gasoline.

Flooded! Not even bothering to swear anymore, she pressed the accelerator all the way to the floor and twisted the key.

After several seconds, the engine coughed, shook, and came unevenly to life. With her foot all the way to the floor, the engine began racing, almost screaming. She switched the lights back on and, letting up a bit on the gas, eased the gear selector into "drive."

There was a short lurch, maybe a yard of forward movement, and silence. Dead again.

Shaking her head in frustration, she snapped off the lights again. The last thing she needed was a dead battery on top of everything else.

Forcing herself to loosen her white-knuckle grip on the steering wheel, she leaned back, her head against the headrest. Maybe if she just let it sit for a few minutes, the trouble would go away, at least long enough to get into town.

Or maybe she should start walking toward the still-lighted house she could see a quarter of a mile down the highway. It was nearly ten, and lights didn't stay on very late around Hazleton, particularly in the countryside.

One more try, and then—

A pair of headlights appeared in the rearview mirror. Someone from Plover's group? Maybe they could give her a lift.

She started to get out of the car, but she stopped uneasily. For the first time in several hours, she remembered the note. And Sandra Forster. Dark country roads, she realized, tended to make such things seem far more real than did well-lighted living rooms.

Hurriedly, before the car could bear down on her in the darkness, she snapped on the emergency flashers. The other car, still a hundred yards or more behind her, seemed to lurch, as if the driver had briefly touched the brakes as Val's flashers came on.

She stayed inside the car but left her window open and stuck her hand out. As she waited for the car to reach her, though, she depressed the door lock.

The oncoming car didn't stop. It merely hesitated briefly before drawing abreast. Then, not even making a rolling stop, it shot out onto the highway and headed toward Hazleton. All Val could see was that a man was driving, and whoever he was, he didn't want to get involved. His car, a medium-sized sedan, was at least as old as Val's Gremlin.

"Thanks, friend," Val muttered to herself as the taillights faded in the distance and vanished around the first curve.

Impatiently, she twisted the key again. As before, the engine started only when she pressed the accelerator to the floor, and it lurched to a stop the instant she put it in gear.

Leaving the flashers going, she got out. She stood by the car long enough to decide not to kick it, and then looked once again toward the lighted farmhouse.

Forcing the thought of the note out of her mind as well as she was able, she started toward the highway a few yards away. She had just reached the berm—crushed gravel next to a shallow, weed-filled ditch—when another car appeared, this one coming from the direction of Hazleton.

She heard its engine change sound as it neared her, and then it was rolling to an easy stop next to her. Val wondered uneasily if it was the same car that had gone past her before, but she quickly saw that it wasn't.

This one was smaller and newer, a two-door, probably red, though it was hard to tell in the light that seeped back from its headlights.

The window on the passenger's side slid down with electric smoothness, and the driver, alone in the car, leaned across the seat toward the open window.

"Car trouble?" he asked. The voice was soft, though a trifle gravelly. She didn't recognize the face that showed dimly in the dash lights.

"Something like that," she said. "It stalled."

"Gas okay?"

"Half full. No, it's something else."

The man was silent a moment, as if considering the situation. Then he shrugged. "Let's take a look at it," he said. "Maybe I can get it started. And if I can't, I can give you a lift to somewhere with a phone."

Without waiting for a reply, he pulled his own car off the highway onto the side road just in front of Val's. The headlights went off almost immediately, replaced by flashers front and back. By the time Val reached the two cars, the man was already climbing out, a small flashlight in one hand. He was, she saw by the pulsing amber of the flashers, fairly young, somewhere in his twenties probably, and a bit less than six feet tall but solidly built. Tightly curling black hair brushed at the collar of the light sport jacket he wore.

"Pop the hood," he said, "and try starting it again. Okay?"

"You don't have to—" she began, but he cut her off.

"It's no trouble, and maybe it's something simple. Go ahead." He laughed, a light chuckle. "And if it needs anything major, think about bringing it in to our shop. We can always use the business."

"Your shop?"

"Oh, sorry. Should've told you. I'm Earl Winters. Bob Wayne and I have a little auto-repair shop down on Fifteenth."

"I hope it's nothing major, but I have been thinking about getting a tune-up sometime before cold weather."

"Our specialty. Look after it myself. Now you just slide in there and let the hood up so I can see what's happening when you start it again." He grinned lopsidedly. "No charge."

A car whizzed by on the highway as Val got in and released the hood. Winters lifted it and leaned over, shining the flashlight here and there. Then he held up one hand. "Hold on a sec. Be right back."

He trotted back to his own car, pulled off his sport jacket and tossed it into the tiny back seat. The dark, short-sleeved pullover sweater he wore revealed that the shoulders weren't the result of padding. His arms were heavy and solidly muscular as he opened the trunk and, after a few metallic clanks, straightened and stuffed a screwdriver and a pair of pliers into his back pocket.

"Okay," he said as he returned to Val's car and shone the flashlight at the engine, "see if you can get it going again."

As before, it acted as if it were flooded, and it would catch only when she jammed the accelerator all the way to the floor. Winters, leaning over and peering here and there with the flashlight, straightened abruptly, waving his hand at her.

"Okay, shut it off," he said.

"See anything?"

"I think so. Looks like your choke's out of whack. Just hang on a sec."

Propping the flashlight in a corner of the engine compartment, Winters leaned down with the screwdriver. He worked silently for a time, the only sound an occasional metal-on-metal clicking.

Abruptly, he straightened, flicking the flashlight off. He stepped back to Val's half open window. "Now try it," he said.

She turned the key. After only a couple of seconds, the engine caught. It still sounded a bit uneven, but it always sounded that way recently. Experimentally, her foot solidly on the brake, she put it in gear.

The car lurched slightly but the engine kept running.

She switched to "park" and turned to Winters. "That seems to have done it, whatever it was," she said, rolling her window down the rest of the way. "Thanks a ton."

"No trouble." He glanced down at his hands. "You don't happen to have some rags or Kleenex or something, do you?"

"Sure, hang on." Leaning across the seat, she pulled open the glove compartment and hauled out a box of tissues. She grabbed a half dozen and handed them out the window. "Here, I've got more if you need them."

He shook his head as he wiped the dirt from his fingers. "You shouldn't have any more trouble with it," he said. "The choke had come loose, somehow, that's all."

"That's a relief. Then it's safe to shut the thing off?"

"Sure. No problem." He began wadding up the tissues. "You sound like you do need a tune-up pretty soon, but that's all. There's nothing wrong that would put you out of operation in the next few miles."

"Here," she said, holding her hand out the window for the wadded up tissues, "I have a litter bag I can put those in."

He hesitated, then handed them to her carefully. "Thanks."

"I'm the one who's indebted," she said, dropping the tissues into the plastic bag suspended from the unused cigarette lighter. "Without your help, I'd still be hiking down the highway looking for a phone. Look, what's the name of your shop? As you said, I do need a tune-up one of these days."

" 'Double-W,' " he said with a faintly sheepish grin. "For Winters and Wayne, or vice versa. Original, huh?"

"At least you didn't call it 'The Dixie Dance King,' " she said, laughing as she recalled the title of one of Burt Reynolds' lesser efforts. "Anyway, do I make an appointment or just bring the car in sometime?"

"I can probably squeeze you in anytime. Helps if you let me know a day or two ahead, though."

"Great. I'll do that. And thanks again."

He waved the thanks away. "No trouble." Hesitantly, he started to back away, toward his own car, but then he stopped.

The faint, self-conscious smile faded, and the barest beginning of a puzzled frown appeared.

"You look familiar," he said uncertainly.

"I'm sorry, I should've introduced myself. I'm Val Hamilton." Shutting off the Gremlin's motor, she stuck her hand out the window. Winters took it, squeezed it briefly. His grip was light, purposely so, Val suspected.

Then, abruptly, the puzzled frown vanished and he snapped his fingers. "The library! Your picture was in the paper a few months ago. I knew I'd seen your face *some*where."

"Maybe in the library itself? Do you get in there often?" Never miss a chance to get in a plug, she added to herself.

Winters shook his head. "Not very often. I don't read a lot. But you've probably seen Sally. That's my wife. She's in there every couple of weeks. But wasn't there something else in the paper about you? You're engaged to Martin Forster, aren't you?"

She laughed shortly. "Yes, there was something in the paper about that, but no, I'm not engaged to him."

"But the paper said—"

"I know. But it was retracted the next day. The whole thing was somebody's idea of a joke."

"A joke?" His frown reappeared, deeper than before. "Who did it?"

"No idea. Someone phoned it in to the paper, someone who *said* he was Martin Forster. Incidentally, do you know Martin?"

"I used to, a little. We were in high school together, but then he went away to college. But you don't have *any* idea who it might have been?"

"Not a one. Martin thinks it's just someone with a sick sense of humor, but he can't imagine who. I don't suppose you have any ideas? You know anyone around Hazleton warped enough to pull a dumb stunt like that?"

He shook his head. "I wish I could help."

"Or someone who might send threatening letters? Or—"

"Letters? What letters?"

"More of the same joke, apparently," she said, and, in a few sentences, told him about the note on Muldoon's collar.

Winters, leaning closer to the open window now, grimaced as he listened, his hard, calloused hands tightening their grip on the window ledge.

"You *have* told the police, haven't you?" he asked sharply when she finished.

She nodded. "Sheriff Lawrence, at any rate."

Winters snorted. "And what's *he* doing about it? Anything?"

"As much as he can, I imagine."

"Which probably isn't much. He's the one who— Look, you *do* know what happened to Martin's wife, don't you? Or didn't anyone bother to tell you?" He sounded angry, but obviously not with her.

"I know she was murdered, if that's what you mean. And that she received a threatening note similar to the one I got."

His eyes widened, as if surprised at the relatively calm way she spoke the words. "That's right," he said. "And they never had even the faintest idea who did it! Whoever it is, he's still out there!" His words were chopped off abruptly, and for a moment he closed his eyes. "Look," he went on, looking down at her earnestly, "I don't want to scare you— No, I think I *do* want to scare you. If I were you, I'd be darned careful for a while. Whoever's doing this may not be the nut who murdered Mrs. Forster, but it's sure a nut of some kind. A nut with a pretty warped sense of humor, if you ask me. And your cat—"

Winters broke off, looking around sharply as the sound of squealing tires came from the highway. As he turned, a car, its headlights on bright, almost skidded around the corner and rocked to a stop only inches from the back bumper of Winters' car. The glaring headlights remained on as the driver's-side door flew open and a tall figure leaped out.

As the figure, jacket flapping, ran through the beams of light from the still running car, Val realized that it was Martin. Before she could say anything, Martin had grabbed Winters by the arm and was trying to jerk him back from the car. Winters, bulkier and stronger despite Martin's four or five inch height advantage, jerked free, holding his arms up defensively.

Val, scrambling out of the car, half shouted: "Martin! Stop it! What do you think you're doing?"

He stopped, suddenly, as if struck over the head. His hands, balled into fists, dropped to his sides. His dark, lean features seemed frozen in a grimace of anger, but abruptly they melted into confusion as his eyes fell on Val. She slammed the car door and moved toward the two men.

"You're all right?" The surprise was plain in Martin's voice.

"I'm fine," she said irritably, "now that Mr. Winters happened along and helped me."

"Helped you? How? He's blocking the road, so you can't—"

"He's not blocking anything!" Val snapped. "My car stalled, and he just now got it started for me again!"

"What was he doing out here?"

"For God's sake, Martin! He was— Look, what are *you* doing out here?"

He shook off the question. "Don't you realize who this is?" He glared at Winters.

"He's Earl Winters, that's who! And he just fixed my car! Now if you don't mind—"

"He was one of the suspects in Sandra's murder!" Martin blurted.

Something cold jerked at her stomach, but then she recovered. "So were you," she shot back. "And Dan Richards and a dozen others."

"I know, but—"

"But *you* were cleared! Well, apparently Mr. Winters was, too! And if you must know, he was just giving me the same kind of warning *you* gave me!" She turned back to the car, grasping the door. "Now if you don't mind, I think I've had enough excitement for one evening."

As she pulled the door open, Martin grasped her arm. She could feel his fingers closing stiffly, almost painfully, even through the fabric of her jacket and blouse. His eyes, only inches from hers, widened. His nose twitched, as if he had gotten a sudden whiff of some offensive odor.

"Martin! Let me go!"

"Where did you—" he began, but Winters' voice, soft but intense, cut him off sharply.

"You heard her, Forster! Let her go!"

Martin's mouth worked silently for a moment, but then, reluctantly, his fingers released their grip. He swallowed audibly as he stepped back. Winters, she saw, had a solid hold on Martin's other arm and was looking at her worriedly.

"You okay, Miss Hamilton?"

She let her breath out in a whoosh, realizing only then that she had been holding it. "I'm all right." She massaged her arm as she looked at Martin, frowning.

"Martin, what's going on? What's the matter with you?"

He shook his head. "It's nothing," he said shortly. "Nothing at all." He glanced at Winters, who was only then releasing his arm warily. He looked back at Val. "You had better go home. As you said, you have certainly had enough excitement for one evening."

"But Martin—" she began, but she stopped as she looked more closely at his face. It held the same mixture of fear and puzzlement she had seen there when the note had been found in Muldoon's collar. And when he had tried to tell her—warn her —about her apparent resemblance to Sandra.

Uneasily, Val got into her car. It started the second she twisted the key. With nodded thanks to Winters, who stood warily to one side and behind Martin, she pulled quickly around their cars and onto the highway.

She did her best not to think—or at least not to worry—about what had happened, but she wasn't totally successful. And the biggest puzzle, as well as the biggest worry, was—how had Martin managed to show up at just that moment? Had he been following her? She didn't see how he could have been, but she didn't see how he could have shown up at precisely that instant, either. And the way he had been acting! The so-called joke must be *really* getting to him. Then sympathy for him overwhelmed her annoyance and puzzlement, and she wondered what she could possibly do to help him. Probably nothing, except to be as understanding as possible, and being understanding was not one of her strong points.

Shaking her head, she reached over and snapped on the car radio, quickly locating the station with the loudest and heaviest rock beat she could find. It helped, at least for the rest of the drive back to town.

At home, she gave Muldoon a late evening snack from his can of crunchies and was about to try to relax with the late show and a peanut butter sandwich—she doubted that she could concentrate enough to read anything, at least not for another few minutes—when the phone rang.

Her mother? It was after eleven, so it was possible, even if it was only three days since her last call. Frowning, she hurried from the kitchen to the living room and located the phone next to the couch where she had left it the last time she'd been talking to Dan.

"Hello?"

"Valerie?"

"Yes, it is. Who— Martin? Is that you?"

"Yes. And please, don't hang up! It's important!"

"I wasn't going to hang up. In fact, I was going to ask you what's going on. I'd still like to know how you happened to show up out there just when you did." So much for understanding, she thought; curiosity wins again.

"I—I was worried," he said, clearly considering her question nothing more than a distraction. "I called your house, but no one answered, and Arlen's said you had already left."

"So you came looking for me?"

"Yes," he snapped, and then added, in a tone of strained apology, "I'm sorry if I upset you, but it cannot be helped. Until this affair is cleared up, one way or another—" He broke off in midsentence, an indication in itself that he was under a strain. His speech was normally composed almost exclusively of complete sentences, and generally grammatically correct ones at that.

Then he was speaking again, in a more subdued but equally tense voice, "I have to ask you about the perfume you were wearing this evening."

"Perfume? What on earth—all right, I'll bite. What about my perfume?"

"What kind was it?"

"I'm not sure. Something from Avon is all I know."

"Avon?"

"One of the library aides back in Milwaukee was an Avon lady one summer, and I was her star customer. Now what's this all about, Martin? Why are you so interested in my perfume all of a sudden?"

"Are you positive what kind of perfume it is?" he asked, ignoring her own questions. "Could you check?"

She frowned at the receiver, but then she shrugged mentally as she reminded herself of the joke and the strain it apparently was putting Martin under. "All right, I'll check. Hang on. I'll be right back."

In the bedroom she found the perfume easily enough. It was right where she had left it, in the middle of the bureau. And it was indeed Avon, but there was no other name on the bottle, which was itself a tiny replica of an old-fashioned Aladdin's lamp, complete with a miniature mantel.

Heading back to the living room, she unscrewed the cap and sniffed—and remembered what she had thought earlier when she had first climbed into the car on the way to Arlen's. Screwing the cap back on, she dropped onto the couch and snatched the receiver up from the cushion where she had dropped it.

"Found it," she said. "It's nameless Avon, in a bottle that looks like one of those old Aladdin's lamps. Now will you tell me what this is all about?"

"You're positive you have the right bottle? You couldn't be mistaken?"

"I'm positive," she snapped, suddenly annoyed at his tone, which struck her as having more than a touch of condescension in it. "Now what's this all about? What's so blasted important about my perfume?"

"Did it smell right to you?"

"*Smell* right? What the—"

"I mean, did it have the same scent tonight that it had the last time you used it?"

She frowned, remembering the lilac scent again. "Not exactly," she admitted, "but I wear it so rarely I can't really be sure. Besides, it's three or four years old and not all that expensive. It's probably changed over the years. Now come on, Martin, what's this all about? What's so important about my perfume all of a sudden?"

She was sure she could hear him swallowing heavily before he answered. "Nothing, I hope. I—I could be wrong, but this evening, at your car, I was positive I—I recognized the scent. I was positive . . ." His voice trailed off maddeningly.

"Yes?" Val prompted impatiently. "You were positive you recognized it. But what did you think it was you recognized?"

Then, abruptly, in the hesitation before he spoke again, Val had an icy feeling that she already had a pretty good idea what the answer was going to be.

And she was right.

"It smelled," he said softly and slowly, "very much like the perfume I bought Sandra on our honeymoon."

Chapter 5

Val wouldn't for a minute let herself seriously consider the possibility that Martin had suggested—that the joker, whoever he was, was responsible for the perfume. That would mean, among other things, that he had been inside her house, and she wasn't ready to even think about something like that. Even so, as she hung up the phone and went to look out the living-room windows, the streetlight seemed a little more distant, the shadows a little deeper.

But even if it *were* true, she thought abruptly, it would prove even more conclusively that Martin rather than herself was the target of the joke. The perfume meant nothing to her, and it probably meant nothing to anyone in all of Hazleton besides Martin Forster.

No, she told herself as firmly as she could manage, the person she should be worrying about was Martin Forster, not herself. The perfume issue aside, he had been acting very strangely, very out of character tonight. He was seeing dangers to Val—and new parts of the "joke"—under every rock. And the perfume probably didn't resemble his wife's nearly as much as he imagined.

Or was she just rationalizing to keep herself from worrying? After all, joke or no joke, she *had* gotten the note.

And Sandra Forster, for whatever reason, *had* been killed.

Shaking her head, she spun away from the windows and snatched up the phone. A few seconds later she was talking to Dan Richards, briefly recounting the evening's events.

She was barely halfway through when he cut in. "I'll be over in five minutes," he said, "as soon as I put my shoes on."

"There's no need—" she began, but he cut her off again.

"Maybe there isn't, but I feel like it. See you in a few minutes." And the line went dead.

She swore as she slammed the receiver down, but then, as she glanced at the silently flickering "Late Show" across the room, she grinned. Why had she tried to argue with him? After an evening like this one, a few minutes of Dan Richards was probably just what she needed.

And it was. During the hour he stayed, they reached no conclusions about Martin's behavior that she hadn't already reached on her own, but it felt good to have someone agree with her.

"Frankly," Dan said at one point, "I think it's just Marty's guilt complex popping up again. God knows, he did everything he logically could be expected to do for Sandra, but he still blames himself for not doing more. I can't say I really blame him for feeling guilty. I probably would, too, logic or no logic. But for five years?" He shook his head. "Anyway, this moronic practical joke is just stirring it all up again for him, and I suppose he wants to be absolutely sure that nothing happens to you the way it did to Sandra. Not that there's any chance of that, but when you're dragging a load of self-imposed guilt like that around . . ." He shrugged.

As for Earl Winters, "he was just another of us suspects." Like the others, he had been put on the list because he was known to have dated Sandra at some time since she had gotten out of high school.

"Never a serious suspect," Dan said. "At least no more serious than I was, maybe even less. As I recall, it was about that time that he got married, just a few days before or after Sandra was killed. So far as I know, he's still amicably, if not happily, married. At least there are no rumors of affairs or divorce, and he flashes pictures of his two kids at anyone who'll look and nod. He didn't show them to you while he was under your hood, did he?"

"In the dark? To a perfect stranger?"

"Wouldn't surprise me. But if you take your car in for him

to work on, you'll no doubt see them. Instead of naked women over the workbench, he's got pictures of his kids."

"You're recommending the 'Double-W,' then?"

"As much as anyplace in town. I've had some stuff done to the Checker there, and it's always been at least satisfactory. Oh, once they screwed something up, but they admitted it and then did it over, no extra charge."

There was more discussion of Sandra—"Sudden unexplained character shifts are not one of my favorite things. I'm even suspicious of those so-called born-again Christians"—and of enemies Martin might have made—"Lawyers can make enemies every time they go into court. The opposition if they win, their own clients if they lose." And then it was well after midnight. Glancing at his watch, Dan stood up abruptly.

"I think," he said, pulling Val to her feet, "that we have run out of constructive ideas, at least for the time being. And I suspect we had best adjourn this meeting for a few hours."

"As you say." She looked up at him, suddenly reluctant to see him leave. "Saturday night still set?"

His heavy eyebrows, as blond as the hair that drooped over his forehead, raised slightly at the question. "Of course. Pick you up at five, show at eight-thirty. Right?" They were driving to South Bend, first for supper and then to see Theodore Bikel, who was on stage at one of the theaters that night.

"Right."

He leaned down in the silence, cupping her face in his hands, and kissed her, lightly at first, then harder as her own hands pressed against the backs of his.

"Everything's going to be all right," he said in a whisper, his lips still touching hers as they moved to form the words.

"I know."

And then he was straightening up, his hands sliding down her neck and shoulders and arms, then closing briefly on her hands. "And I'll talk to Marty in the morning. I'll see if he knows something he's not telling us."

Instead of following him to the door, Val walked to the living-room windows and watched as he went down the narrow

walkway to the sidewalk, turned to twitch his right hand in a
wave, and hurried across the street to where his Checker stood
like a large, red box on wheels. As he dug his keys from his
trouser pocket and raised them toward the lock, he stopped.

For a moment it seemed that he was going to turn away from
the car, but then his motion with the keys continued and he
unlocked and opened the door. The engine caught and the
Checker lumbered away.

Five minutes later, just as Val was starting to put toothpaste
on the brush, the doorbell rang. Frowning, she screwed the cap
back on the tube and, refastening all but a couple of the buttons on her blouse, she hurried down the hall to the living-room
window that looked out on the small front step. Cautiously, she
peered through the crack in the drapes.

Her frown deepened as she saw Dan Richards standing there,
one hand firmly gripping the arm of a middle-aged, slightly
heavyset, balding man in a rumpled suit. What the devil was
going on *now?*

Hastily fastening the last two buttons and stuffing the bottom
of the blouse into the waist of the skirt, she opened the door a
crack. Before she could say anything, Dan asked abruptly,
"Val, do you know this man?"

Startled at the sudden question, she looked at the man
blankly a second before she flipped on the outside light. She
shook her head. "I don't think so. Who is he?"

"That's what I'm trying to find out." Dan glowered at the
man as well as he could, though his large blue eyes and pleasant face were obviously not the best raw material for a truly
menacing glower. The man remained silent and motionless, as
if neither of the others existed.

Dan moved a step backward, pulling the man with him.
"That's his car across the street," he said, pointing, "a couple
doors down. Does *that* look familiar?"

Deftly blocking Muldoon, who had heard the door open and
was trying to slip past her legs, Val eased herself out onto the
front step and looked where Dan was pointing with his free
hand. The car was a dark sedan, not particularly distinctive,

probably five or six years old. The rear license plate was smudged and partly illegible in the dim light from the street-lamp. She started to shake her head, but then she stopped, frowning.

She looked at the man again, the way he hunched forward, head down, as if trying to escape from the light.

A chill shot through her.

"I can't be positive," she said slowly, "but that *may* be the car that passed me when I stalled this evening."

Dan nodded. "Interesting. And he's been parked over there—watching your house, I'd guess—for quite a while. I saw him when I drove up, and he was still there when I left."

The chill deepened as the possibilities raced through her mind. Had the problem with her car not been an accident? Had this man been waiting out there tonight until Dan left? Until she was alone?

"Call the sheriff, Val," Dan said quietly, his fingers tightening on the other's arm.

The man stiffened. "No, wait."

"Why should we wait?" Dan asked sharply.

The man swore under his breath, a series of resigned sounding expletives. "Look, lady, you're Valerie Hamilton, aren't you?"

"Yes, but who are you?"

"My name is Carl Jacobs. Look, can we go inside?"

"Why were you watching her house?" Dan asked, ignoring the man's question.

Jacobs sighed, shaking his balding head. "All right, all right. Whatever you say. We'll stand on the front steps all night if that's your thing. Just don't call the cops. The last thing I need is trouble with local cops. I'm a private investigator, from Indianapolis. My ID is in my wallet, if you'll let me get it."

"Where? Back pocket?"

"Yeah, that's the place." The man sighed again, this time with a touch of amusement. "You want to get it out yourself? Be my guest. My only gun is in the glove compartment of the car, by the way."

Hesitantly, Dan shifted his grip on Jacobs' arm and cautiously reached under the man's jacket, wrinkled from hours of sitting in the car, and came out with a wallet. It was as battered and tired looking as Jacobs. Dan tossed it to Val, who realized what he was doing barely in time to catch it.

"In the plastic holders," Jacobs said, "next to the drivers' license."

She found it, along with several credit cards, a library card, and some faded photos of a youngish looking woman and a couple of boys, maybe ten or twelve years old. Behind the license itself was a card with Jacobs' name in one corner, along with the legend: "Hoosier State Detective Agency, Confidential Surveillances, Missing Persons, Insurance and Industrial Work."

Val handed the wallet to Dan, who held it up to the light and looked at the card.

"All right, Mr. Jacobs," he said, "I assume this falls under the 'confidential surveillance' heading. Who hired you? And why?"

Another tired sigh. "And if you don't like my answers, you'll still call your friend the sheriff."

"That's right."

Jacobs scraped his free hand across his forehead and the few strands of hair that remained on the top of his head. "This puts me in an awkward position. You know that."

"I know and I don't particularly care."

A snort of almost-laughter. "I didn't think you would, somehow. Look, will you let me phone the guy who hired me?"

"Not until you tell us who he is."

Jacobs looked briefly at Dan, as if gauging his strength. Dan's grip tightened on his arm.

"All right. Considering why I'm watching you—all right. Someone named Martin Forster hired me. Now can I call him?"

"Martin Forster?" It was almost a chorus as Dan and Val stared at the man, wide-eyed.

"You're positive about that?" Val asked. "Did you actually see him?"

Jacobs looked offended. "Of course."

Dan eyed the man thoughtfully. "All right," he said abruptly, "inside! Val, call Marty and ask him to get over here. Don't tell him why. Don't even hint."

Jacobs made a slight flinching motion and shook his head, but he said nothing.

Chapter 6

Martin's dark gray Cadillac lurched to a stop at the curb in front of Val's house. Martin, tieless and in his shirt sleeves, leaped out almost before the car had stopped bouncing on its expensive springs. For an instant, as he rounded the rear of the car, he faltered, and his eyes seemed to jerk to a halt as they passed over Jacobs' nondescript sedan across the street. Then he was dashing across the lawn to the front door.

He jerked the screen door open and, ignoring the bell, pounded loudly on the door. He was rattling the knob futilely when Val opened the door.

Looking down at her, he blinked. His breathing was rapid, his face flushed.

"Val! Are you all right? What's wrong?"

"I don't know," she said quietly. "Come on in, Martin. There's someone here I'd like you to meet."

"Who—" Martin's voice came to a stop as suddenly as if he had been guillotined. His face froze, mouth partially open, as Dan maneuvered Jacobs into Martin's line of sight.

Anger replaced the shock on Martin's face. "Jacobs! What are you doing in *here?*"

"This guy spotted me," Jacobs said in a flat voice. "I'm sorry, but it happens. And you can't say I didn't warn you."

"Then this *is* the man who hired you?" Dan asked.

"Of course. Martin Forster, right?"

Val, nudging Martin the rest of the way through the door, closed it behind him. Muldoon, unperturbed by a houseful of people, was sprawled hopefully on the floor near one end of the couch.

"All right," Val said, "would *someone* care to take a shot at explaining what this is all about? Martin?"

When Martin remained uncomfortably silent, she leaned closer, looking up at him angrily. "Well? For a start, was this character you hired following me around out at Arlen's tonight? Is *that* how you showed up, Johnny on the Spot?"

Jacobs sighed. "You better tell her, Forster. The way things are now, she thinks I sabotaged her car."

"What?" Martin blinked. "Did someone do something to your car? Is that why it stalled?"

"Not unless your friend here did it! Now come on, Martin! Quit all this beating around the bush. *What is going on?*"

Reluctantly, with a mixture of embarrassment and defiance, Martin explained. Stripped of all embellishments and diversions, the reason was simplicity itself. Martin, worried about the lengths to which the so-called joker might go, had hired Jacobs' agency to keep a protective eye on Val. Since the subject wasn't supposed to know she was being watched or protected, there had been problems from the start, and Jacobs was almost glad the affair was out in the open at last.

"I told you it was impossible to do a proper job of protecting someone as long as you insist on keeping it a deep, dark secret," Jacobs said.

"I could've told you that myself, Martin," Val snapped. Then her voice softened. "Look, I appreciate the thought, but if you want to hire a detective, you'd be better off hiring him to try to find out who's doing these crazy things."

"That was part of my purpose, too," Martin said hastily. "I thought that if he watched the house, he might—" He stopped abruptly.

"Yes?" Val prompted. "In case anyone *else* is lurking around my house, your detective might see who it is?"

Martin nodded uncomfortably.

"Well, I didn't see anyone like that," Jacobs said. "And unless Miss Hamilton here consents to my continued presence, there's no point in any further attempts at surveillance, protective or otherwise." There was a sarcastic tinge to the last words.

"What's that supposed to mean?" Martin bristled at the tone. "I told you why you were hired. If you can't handle the job—"

"I know what you told me. All I'm telling you now is it can't be done. On the other hand, if what you really want is a record of everyone with whom she comes in contact, that's another matter altogether." Jacobs' eyes rested briefly, suggestively, on Dan.

Martin's eye widened as he realized what Jacobs was implying. "It's not like that at all!" he protested angrily.

"Then why keep it a secret from Miss Hamilton?"

"Because," Val put in, "he knows I wouldn't put up with it if I knew about it, that's why."

Jacobs looked at Val. "You don't want protection, then?"

"I can do without *this* kind, thank you!"

Jacobs shrugged. "Then as far as my involvement is concerned, that would seem to be the end of that. I'll send you a bill in the morning, Mr. Forster."

"But you can't quit now!"

"I don't have much choice. All Miss Hamilton has to do is call the police and have me picked up."

"I'd tell them who you are, that you're working for me!"

Jacobs shook his head. "Sorry. Unless you get the police—or Miss Hamilton herself—to agree to this, there's nothing I can do. The last thing I need is trouble with police. It's very easy to lose a license, very easy."

Martin sucked his breath in as if he were going to begin another protest, but then he wilted, his shoulders slumping. "Very well, Mr. Jacobs. Send me your bill."

Jacobs glanced briefly at Dan, then Val. "I'm sorry if I caused you any trouble or frightened you." He pulled one of his cards from his shirt pocket and handed it to Val. "If you change your mind for any reason . . ." he said, letting his voice trail off.

Val took the card, glanced at it and dropped it on the coffee table in front of the couch. Jacobs shrugged as his eyes followed the card. With a final nod to Martin, he left. The opening and closing of the door was loud in the otherwise silent house, and his footsteps were plainly audible as he made his way heavily down the walk to the street and his car.

"I think," Dan said, reaching out to take Martin's arm, "it's time to call it a night. We could all use a little rest."

They started across the room toward the door, but Martin stopped abruptly, almost literally digging his heels into the carpet.

"No!" he said sharply, turning toward Val. "There's more—more that you have to know! Especially now!"

"Come on, Marty," Dan said, trying unsuccessfully to sound soothing as he continued to urge Martin toward the door, "it's been a long day. We can all get together tomorrow and talk about it."

Dan's tone made Martin stiffen all the more. He shook his head. "No, now! After the perfume, it can't wait any longer!"

Dan started to speak again, but Val interrupted. "It's all right. I don't think I could sleep now, anyway. I'd just as soon get everything straightened out right now."

Dan frowned. "Val told me about the perfume, Marty. The scent apparently changed, but that's all it was. Perfume does that, you know."

Martin shook his head doggedly. "It didn't just 'change scent,'" he said, and his tone was that of an adult lecturing a backward child. "Can't you understand that? It was the same perfume I gave Sandra two days after we were married! Don't you think I would even recognize *that*, for God's sake?"

"Frankly, no," Dan said, holding his hand up to ward off the protests. "Marty, that was five years ago. And perfumes aren't all that distinctive. I can't tell My Sin from Chanel Number 83, or whatever the number is, and I doubt that many men can."

"So you think I imagined it? Is that it? I don't blame you, but—"

"I didn't say that. Sure, the perfume changed. Val noticed it, too, but that's all it is. Just a change."

Martin continued to shake his head in stubborn denial.

"All right," Dan said, his voice as flat and calm as he could make it, "what's *your* theory? Are you saying that our practical joker actually got into this house? *Broke* in? And poured Val's perfume out of the bottle and substituted a different perfume? Is that it?"

"I don't have any idea of the specific details," Martin said. "All I know is it *was done!* And it isn't the first thing that's happened!" The last words came out in a rush.

"The note and the engagement, you mean?" Dan said. "We know all about—"

"That's *not* what I mean!"

"What, then? Nothing else has happened."

"Nothing else that you know about, you mean!" Martin hesitated, as if reluctant even now to continue.

"What else has happened, Martin?" Val's voice was quiet, but a nervous tingling was playing over her skin. "And whatever it is, why haven't you told us before?"

He shook his head. "I was afraid to. I was afraid perhaps I *was* imagining it."

"What are you talking about, for God's sake?" Dan prompted irritably, and Val put a restraining hand on Dan's arm.

Martin swallowed. "It's happened a half-dozen times in the last few weeks. I wake up in the middle of the night—two or three in the morning—and I can smell that perfume—Sandra's perfume!—in the air."

Dan snorted. "Dreams, Marty, nightmares! Come on!"

Martin laughed, a short, brittle bark. "Believe me, I know how it sounds. And I told myself the very same thing, not once but a hundred times! That's why I haven't told anyone about it before. That's why I haven't done anything but worry—and hire a detective." His eyes came to rest on Val. His face hardened.

"But that's not all," he went on. "The last time—last Sunday night, the night before that announcement appeared in the paper, if you want to be specific about it!—there was more than perfume. There was music. And I do not mean 'ghostly music floating ethereally in the midnight air!' I mean *real* music! A record, being played on *my* stereo just two rooms away!"

Martin fell silent, and Dan, a touch of sarcasm in his voice, said, "And I suppose it was Sandra's voice on the record."

"No, it wasn't!" Martin snappped angrily. "But it *was* a record she owned, a record she'd gotten just a couple of weeks before we were married! And it was a song she had been trying to learn—*from that very record!*" He blinked and fell silent again, this time turning away from them both.

Val started to reach out and touch his arm, but he pulled away. His back was still to them, his face toward the broad, living-room windows. "I know how it sounds," he said, his voice unsteady. "I thought the same thing the next morning. I told myself I was having a nervous breakdown, that I was hallucinating, whatever! But the record was still there, next to the record player, precisely where I had left it! And that blasted perfume was still in the air!"

"You're making it sound like a ghost story!" Dan snapped.

"I told you, I *know* what it sounds like! If it weren't for the note and the announcement in the paper, I *would* think I was losing my mind. But those—they are too solid to be imagination."

"All right," Val said. "What you're saying is that whoever got into your house and did those things has gotten into *my* house, too."

"That must be what happened."

"Then let's just see if anything *else* has been disturbed," she said. Her voice was calmer than she felt as she turned and made her way into the hall. "Come on, we might as well start with the rest of the perfume."

They followed her, saying nothing.

The first thing they discovered was that three bottles of perfume, not just one, had "changed scent." And all three scents were, as far as any of them could tell, identical. All were the pungent lilac that Martin insisted was identical to Sandra's perfume.

For the first time, then, Val truly believed that someone *had* been in the house. She shivered as she put the last bottle back in the box in the bureau drawer. Dan stood close behind her, his hands gripping her shoulders, offering what comfort he could.

"At least," Val said, "whoever it was must have been here in the daytime, not at night. I'm a light sleeper, and I don't think this could have been done without waking me or setting off Muldoon."

The thought of someone moving silently past her bed to the bureau made her shiver again. "In any event," she said, "I think I'm going to fasten those chain latches after this. Even if whoever did this has a key, the chains should keep him out." She laughed nervously. "And to think, one of the reasons I had for moving to a small town was so I wouldn't have to worry about burglars."

Then, as she looked through her jewelry drawer—necklaces, earrings, pins, and a few rings—she found an item she didn't recognize. Frowning, she brought it out and held it up, turning it in the light as she looked at it. It was a pin, in the shape of a butterfly, perhaps an inch across, the color of gold but probably made of brass. The wings, embossed with intricate designs on the upper surfaces, were arched. The body, too, was embossed, and a pair of fairly realistic looking antennae sprouted from the head. The wings, though, were what held her attention. The embossed patterns were not symmetrical. Each wing was different. Then, as her mind shifted gears, the way it sometimes did when she looked at an optical illusion, the patterns became clear. Buried in each wing was an ornate, gothic-style letter. "S" on the left wing, "H" on the right.

"This isn't mine," she said, turning toward the two men, who had been standing silently, watching as she searched and sorted.

As she held it out, Martin took it in his hand and held it up to the light. His expression didn't change, but the color drained from his face.

Val swallowed nervously. "From the way you look, I assume that pin means something to you."

He nodded slowly, his face still pale. "Yes," he said, barely above a whisper. "It belonged to Sandra."

A renewed chill shot through Val as Martin's hushed voice seemed to echo in her mind. Then, before she could get her thoughts in order, Dan took the pin from Martin.

"How can you be sure it's hers?" he asked. "It doesn't look all that distinctive."

"Her initials," he said. "You can see them on the wings. 'S' and 'H.' Sandra Haynes—her name before we were married."

"You're positive this is the same pin?" Dan asked sharply. "Absolutely positive?"

"As positive as I *can* be." Martin's gaze was fastened on the pin in Dan's hand as if he were being hypnotized.

Dan nodded. "All right, maybe we're getting somewhere at last. Who owns this pin now? Who was it given to after your wife died?"

Martin, still gazing blankly at the pin, said nothing. Dan reached out and gripped his shoulder lightly. "Marty? Are you okay?"

Martin blinked. His eyes came into focus again. "What? What was that?"

"I asked, who got this pin after your wife died?"

"Her sister," Martin said, scowling. "Thelma Jeskie. She has everything."

"She should still have the pin, then?"

Martin shook his head irritably. "How should I know? I haven't seen it for five years. All I know is, Thelma took all the jewelry. I . . . didn't want it around."

"Nothing was sold?"

Martin snorted. "Not unless Thelma did the selling. But what difference does any of this make?"

Dan's eyebrows went up. "Don't you see? If this really *is* the same pin, then we had better talk to this Thelma Jeskie and find out what she did with the pin. Did she sell it? Give it away? If so, to whom?"

Martin shook his head sharply. "There's no point in talking to her."

Dan frowned, as did Val. "I don't understand, Marty. If Thelma Jeskie is the last person you know of who had this pin

—even if it *was* five years ago—then she's the logical place to start if we're going to try to trace it and find out how it ended up in Val's bureau."

"I don't care if you understand or not," Martin snapped. "There is no point in talking to Thelma Jeskie. No point at all!"

Nothing Val or Dan said could budge Martin on the subject of Thelma Jeskie. It was as if the very mention of her name brought an iron door clanging shut in his mind, and when they persisted, he turned and stalked out of the house.

As they watched him climb unsteadily into his car and lurch away from the curb, Val looked up at Dan. "I don't know about you," she said, "but that little performance makes me all the more anxious to talk to Thelma Jeskie."

Chapter 7

With the chains on both front and back doors fastened and all window latches checked, Val got a fair night's sleep despite waking up at least a dozen times, including every time Muldoon thumped to the floor anywhere in the house or batted one of his toys, even the soft, catnip-stuffed variety, against the walls or furniture.

Shortly after eleven the next day—a brisk, almost chilly Friday—Val, wearing her dark conservative slacks and blouse under a warm but not so conservative green poncho, stood at the door of the Jeskies' small, frame house. It was in Elmwood Heights, one of the older—and now one of the more run-down—additions to Hazleton. The Jeskie house was typical fifties' construction, small and boxy with a carport on one side. It looked recently painted, and the lawn was neatly mowed with only one or two autumn dandelions marring its smoothness.

There were heavy footsteps from inside the house almost the instant Val pressed the doorbell. The door popped open, and a short, slightly overweight man in dark green, heavily smudged work clothes, looked out. His eyes widened in friendly surprise and a smile spread across his rounded, almost pudgy face.

"You're the new librarian, aren't you? Miss Hamilton, isn't it?" Seeing her look of surprise, he rushed on. "I haven't goofed, have I? I mean, I saw your picture in the paper when you came to town, and—" He stopped, shaking his head and laughing. "What can I do for you, whether you're Miss Hamilton or not?"

Val found herself wanting to laugh with him. "Yes, I'm Valerie Hamilton. And you're Mr. Jeskie?"

He nodded. "Just call me Wally. Now, like I said, what can I do for you?"

"Is Mrs. Jeskie home?"

"Thel? Sure, come on in. We just finished lunch, and she'd— I work over at the foundry, you know, out on Second Street. Or I suppose you don't know, really. Anyway, like I started to say, I always come home for lunch. It's real handy, only a mile or so away. Not like the big cities, where you have to drive a half hour each way. Or take a train or something like that. Real handy."

By the second "real handy," Wally Jeskie had led the way through the living and dining rooms and into the kitchen. A thin, dark-haired woman, somewhere in her twenties, was scraping dishes in the sink and putting them into an already half-full automatic dishwasher.

Jeskie laughed as he glanced at the open dishwasher. "We just sort of save them up until we get enough for a full load," he said. "With just the two of us, we don't get that many dirty. And we save energy by doing them all at the same time. Or so they tell us."

The woman looked around, a disapproving look tightening her already sharp features.

"Hon," Jeskie said, "this is Miss Valerie Hamilton. You know, the librarian they got to replace Flora. Miss Hamilton, this is my wife, Thelma."

For a moment, Thelma's face remained frozen in the same mixture of surprise and disapproval. Then, as if with a great effort, she brought forth a faint smile.

"I'll leave you two alone," Jeskie said, still smiling. "I gotta get back to work." He leaned toward his wife, gave her a quick, noisy kiss, and disappeared through the kitchen door with a wave and a "See you this evening, hon."

As the door slammed, even the faint smile disappeared from the woman's face. "What brings you here, Miss Hamilton?" she asked as she picked up the last of the dishes, rinsed it, and set it carefully into the dishwasher and closed the door. "You aren't collecting for something, are you?"

"Collecting? No, of course not. I—"

"Flora did that a lot, you know. She was always involved in some charity or other."

"No, this is nothing like that," Val said, trying not to sound as ill at ease as she suddenly felt, subjected to this woman's scrutiny. She seemed as cold and hostile as her husband had been warm and friendly.

"Might as well go in the other room," Thelma said indifferently, "whatever it is you want."

Not bothering to remove the apron from over the rather plain print dress she wore, the woman led the way back into the living room and lowered herself tiredly onto the couch in front of the picture window that looked out on the narrow side yard. Val remained standing for a moment before seating herself tentatively in a chair facing Thelma Jeskie.

"I understand you're Sandra Forster's sister."

The woman's narrow face stiffened even more. "Sandra *Haynes'* sister, yes."

Apparently the feeling between Martin and his sister-in-law was mutual. It did not look as if talking to her would be easy.

"Yes," Val agreed, "Sandra Haynes. She was married to Martin Forster."

"For a few days," Thelma Jeskie said coldly.

Obviously there was to be no small talk or gossip, Val thought. Might as well get right to it. She opened her purse and took out the pin. She leaned forward and held it out for Thelma to see. The woman frowned the instant her eyes focussed on it. She looked up at Val, her eyes narrowing suspiciously.

"Where did you get that?" Her voice was as accusing as her eyes.

"I was hoping you might be able to help me find out," Val said, using her most soothing voice, the one usually reserved for particularly irritated patrons at the library.

"Help *you* find out? I don't understand."

"I don't either, believe me. That's why I'm here." Very briefly, Val explained. Thelma listened intently, the tight frown not relaxing for even an instant. "This pin is the first really concrete thing we've had to go on. I understand it might have been part of the jewelry you got from your sister after her death," Val finished.

"And you're accusing *me* of breaking into your house and 'planting' it in your bedroom?"

"No, no, of course not!" Val said hastily. "I just wanted to find out for sure if this is the same pin. And if it is, I was hoping you might be able to help me trace it to whoever *did* plant it in my house."

Slowly, the frown still in place, Thelma took the pin from Val's outstretched fingers. She turned it in the light from the broad window behind her. As she held it close to her face, her eyes taking in every detail, she seemed to be remembering it more than studying it. Finally she nodded.

"Yes, this is the same pin."

"Can you be sure? Just from the initials?"

"It's more that that." Thelma held the pin out, pointing to something on the underside of one of the wings. "Those little scratches there. You see them?"

Val nodded, and Thelma went on. "The catch didn't work. It was too loose. Wally fixed it, but his pliers slipped and scratched it. Right there."

Val leaned close and looked. There were two tiny gouges in the metal, so small as to be unnoticeable unless they were pointed out. When she looked up, she was surprised to see the beginnings of a smile pulling at the corners of Thelma Jeskie's mouth.

"And you say that dear Martin took the joke rather badly?" Thelma's tone, if not her actual lip, curled as she spoke Martin's name.

"He seemed upset, yes. But I can't say that I blame him, being reminded of his wife's death that way."

Thelma's smile broadened. There was amusement in the smile, but still it was hard and brittle. Then her eyes met Val's, and she laughed aloud. "I wish I could've seen his face."

Val frowned puzzledly. "*Did* you plant this pin? And do those other things?"

Val half expected an angry explosion, but Thelma only shook her head, still smiling.

"No," she said, "I didn't. But I wish I had. I truly wish I had thought of them, but I didn't. No, that pin, along with a number of other items, were stolen some time ago. A month, at least."

"I don't understand," Val said. "Why would you want to play a joke like that on Martin?"

Thelma laughed again, but then fell abruptly silent, her face somber now. "No," she said, "I didn't think you would understand." She shrugged. "It's really very simple. Martin Forster murdered my sister. Someone apparently has finally decided to believe me and is doing something about it."

There was a stunned silence. No wonder Martin didn't want to talk to Thelma, Val thought. Keeping her voice as neutral as she could, she asked, "What makes you think he killed her?"

"You're sure you want to know?"

Val nodded. "Very much."

Thelma shrugged again, leaning back in the corner of the couch. "As you like. Again, it's simplicity itself. You do know what the popular theory is, don't you?"

"That she was killed by one of her former boyfriends who was jealous because she married Martin?"

"That's the one. Well, it's wrong. One hundred percent wrong."

"But why would Martin want to kill her? They had only been married a week or two as I understand it. And the threats—"

"The threats were simply to make it *look* as if a jealous boyfriend did it. As for why, I'll bet no one has told you—I'll certainly bet *Martin Forster* hasn't told you—that Sandra had been pregnant a few months before they were married? And that she had had an abortion?"

"No, no one told me. But how is that a reason for Martin to kill her?"

"If you knew your dear Martin a little better . . ." The anger was rising in Thelma's face, in her voice.

"Was Martin the father?"

Thelma laughed bitterly. "If he had been, Sandy would be alive today. No, it was someone else. I don't know who, and it doesn't matter."

"I still don't understand."

"All right, you want to understand? I'll tell you so you'll be sure to understand." Another harsh laugh. "I'm sure you've heard how Mr. Straight-Arrow Forster, with his fine moral influence, 'reformed' poor Sandra."

"I'd heard that he *thought* something like that," Val said noncommittally.

"Exactly. He thought it, and he gloried in it, the self-righteous bastard!"

"What are you suggesting? That he didn't have anything to do with her reforming? Or that she didn't reform?"

"Oh, she 'reformed,' all right. I wish to God she hadn't, but she did. You don't think that stuffed-shirt Forster would marry anyone who didn't have the highest moral character, do you?"

Val shrugged but said nothing.

"But it wasn't Forster who reformed her," Thelma went on, her voice still bitter. "It was the pregnancy and the abortion. I don't know if she waited too long, if she got a bad doctor at the clinic she went to, or what. But whatever happened, it shocked her, scared her half to death. She was a different person when she came back from Chicago. A completely different person." She shook her head sadly. "The sort of person who would marry a creep like Martin Forster!"

"But you still haven't told me what any of this has to do with Martin being the one who killed her," Val prompted when Thelma fell silent, staring blankly into the distance. "Didn't he know what she had been like before? You're certainly not saying he discovered—"

"No, he knew. He knew very well, or he couldn't have taken credit for reforming her, now could he?" Thelma's voice was heavy with sarcasm. "He had always been the first to look down his nose at her or to make an insulting remark about her. He knew what she had been like."

"Then what—"

"The only thing he *didn't* know about was the pregnancy. And the abortion. I'm probably the only one that Sandra told. The only one." Thelma's thin face softened, and tears glistened in the corners of her eyes for an instant before she brushed them roughly away. "But then she told *him!* After they were engaged, she told *him!*"

"How do you know?"

"She told me she was going to. Her new conscience was bothering her." Thelma laughed harshly. "As if she had any responsibility to tell him anything! I told her to keep it to herself, the way she had up till then, but she wouldn't listen. She just wouldn't listen. She was positive that the saintly Martin Forster would understand and forgive her. And that if he wouldn't, then she didn't deserve to be forgiven!"

"But that still doesn't explain why you think he would want to kill her."

Thelma snorted derisively. "Don't you see how his mind would work? He was engaged to her, the announcement had been made publicly, he was committed. And then she told him about the abortion. And he couldn't take it. That was a little too real, too concrete for him to take. Lots of boyfriends, a bad reputation, those kinds of things he could take, particularly since he'd convinced himself that he personally was the reason she'd given them up. But a pregnancy? An abortion? No way. It was just too much for him. So what are his choices? He can call off the engagement, but then he'd have to explain why. And he'd look like a fool to everyone. Even *he* must have realized he'd look like a pompous jackass, handing down moral judgments like that. And, like most pompous jackasses, he was convinced that the whole world circulated around him and that he would never, ever live it down."

Thelma pulled in a deep breath and let it out in a noisy sigh. "So he killed her. He made up those threats to make it look like one of her boyfriends killed her out of jealousy, and he killed her. He changed himself—he thought—from a pompous jackass to a bereaved widower."

Thelma looked up at Val from where she was slumped back on the couch. There were tears in the woman's eyes again, and this time she didn't bother to brush them away. "But *I* know that he's still a pompous jackass. And a murderer!"

When Val pulled into her parking spot behind the blocky brick building that was the Hazleton Public Library, a frowning Sheriff Mel Lawrence climbed quickly from his car, slamming the door loudly. He was standing next to Val's door, looming over her as she climbed out.

"I thought I told you to let me know if anything—anything at all—happened!" he said angrily as she managed to open the door far enough to ease herself all the way out.

"I was going to," she said defensively. "In fact, I was going to call you as soon as I got inside."

"Twelve hours *after* these things happened?"

She blinked. "Oh, the perfume!" In the aftermath of Thelma Jeskie's accusations, she had forgotten the perfume and the pin, which was what had started the whole thing.

"Yes, the perfume! And the pin! What did you think I was talking about?" He eyed her suspiciously.

"Martin's been to see you already, then? He's told you everything?"

"Including the fact that your car stalled for no reason. Don't forget that."

His brusque, accusing tone was beginning to irritate her, or at least to take her off the defensive. "Don't worry, I won't," she snapped. "Did he tell you about the detective he hired, too?"

He nodded, running his stubby fingers through his curling, reddish hair. "He did. He also said you wouldn't have anything to do with the man. Now if you don't mind my saying so, you might have been better off letting him stay on the job. He couldn't do any harm, and he just might have been able to help."

"Now you're saying I *need* someone to guard me? The last time I talked to you, you were convinced that it was all a joke—on Martin—and that I was perfectly safe."

Lawrence looked harassed. "I know what I said, and I don't think I ever said you were *perfectly* safe. Oh, you probably *are* safe, but it's foolish to take chances. And to turn down any protection you're offered!"

"All right, all right. Maybe you're right. But something else has come up, and—"

"What? Another threat?"

She shook her head impatiently. "No, not another threat. It's just something that contradicts what Dan told me about Martin being the only one with a perfect alibi for Sandra's murder. Have you ever talked to Thelma Jeskie?"

He looked puzzled, then annoyed at the sudden change of subject. "Don't tell me *you've* been talking to her?"

"Just a few minutes ago. I went to ask her about the pin, since she was supposed to have gotten it from Sandra. But she—"

"You thought she might be the one who planted it in your house? That she might even be responsible for the other things that happened?"

"She said she wasn't, and she said the pin—and some other jewelry she'd gotten from her sister—had been stolen a few weeks ago. Or they turned up missing, at least. But considering how she feels about Martin—"

"I take it she told you her theory of what happened to Mrs. Forster, then?"

"You know about it?"

Lawrence sighed tiredly. "I know about it," he said, and then went on in an almost singsong voice: "Martin Forster killed his wife because he found out she had had an abortion a few months before they were married. He just didn't have the guts to break it off and admit he'd made a mistake in ever wanting to marry her, so he killed her in order to save face. Does that about cover it? Or has she added some embellishments now?"

Val blinked, leaning back against the hood of her car. She nodded up at Lawrence. "That's about it. From your tone, I assume you don't believe a word of it."

"Oh, the abortion part is true. The autopsy showed that.

And her 'conversion' is probably true, too. At least it could be. An abortion is a pretty traumatic thing to go through, particularly in a strange city. Even more particularly if there's no one to go with you to hold your hand."

"The father didn't go with her?"

Lawrence shook his head. "According to Thelma, whoever the father was, he probably didn't even know she was pregnant. For that matter, Sandra may not have known who the father was."

Val shivered inwardly, trying to imagine for a moment what it must have been like, alone in a strange city, putting herself in the impersonal hands of doctors and nurses she had never seen before and would never see again after that day. And the abortion itself, no matter what a woman's personal convictions, had to be a severe shock, both mental and physical.

For the first time, Val saw Sandra as a real person and not just a face in a snapshot or a story in a newspaper. Even when Dan—and Martin—had talked about her, she had remained distant and unreal, a collection of statistics and opinions rather than a living, breathing human being. But now, suddenly, as she imagined Sandra's lonely ordeal—

Abruptly, Val shook her head, as if the physical action could jar the thoughts from her mind. "I take it you don't put much faith in Mrs. Jeskie's accusation of Martin."

"None at all. She's been making it from the day her sister was killed, and no one's been able to change her mind."

"Not even Martin's airtight alibi?"

"Not even that."

"What *is* this alibi, incidentally? Dan mentioned it the other day, but he didn't tell me what it was."

There was a pause, and then, with a trace of annoyance, Lawrence said, "*I'm* the alibi."

"You?"

"Yes, me. Me and the whole county board."

"What happened?" Val persisted, ignoring his obvious reluctance.

He sucked in his breath and looked away from her, toward

the massive, columned church across the street from the library. He didn't look back at her as he spoke.

"I screwed up," he said, his voice low but with a biting edge. "I screwed up! That's what happened!"

Then the emotion was forcefully submerged. "Sorry," he said. "It's not your fault." He closed his eyes a second, and when he opened them, still not looking at her, he began speaking again. The words sounded as if they had been said many times, to many people.

"Right at the end, Sheriff Hyatt—I was a deputy then—started taking the threats seriously. Seriously enough to have a twenty-four-hour-a-day guard set up, at least for a few days. I don't know how long it could've been kept up; probably not very long, not on our budget. Anyway, I had the evening shift. Forster was at a county board meeting, so Mrs. Forster and I were alone. I heard something outside the house, in the back yard, so I went out to investigate. Gun drawn and everything, careful as I could be, which obviously wasn't careful enough!" Gradually his voice had filled with self-directed sarcasm. "Not nearly careful enough! Someone caught me from behind, just like the worst amateur. Hit me with a club of some sort, I suppose. And that's the last I remember until Forster was standing over me, shaking me and screaming, 'What happened? What happened?'"

Lawrence had almost been shouting himself, his round face starting to flush.

"And Martin's alibi?" Val asked into the silence.

"Simple. It was all down in black and white, as they say. According to the official minutes, the board meeting didn't end until nine-fifty. And Forster was the last speaker. And before you ask the universal question, how did I know exactly when I was knocked out, that's all down in black and white, too, just like the minutes of the meeting. I was a real junior G-man in those days. I kept notes and everything. You can see the notebook if you want. It's around somewhere, I'm sure, stashed in one of the filing cabinets. Nothing ever gets dumped around here except people. The entry says, 'Noise in subject's back yard, 9:37. Going to investigate.' " He shrugged. "And that's it. Unless Forster and I were working together to kill his wife—which Mrs. Jeskie *has* suggested, more than once—Martin's totally in the clear."

There was a long silence. Then Val said, "I'm sorry."

"For what? For wanting to know the truth? Don't be. It's certainly not your fault that I still get guilt twinges for being dumb enough to—to do what I did." He straightened abruptly and turned to look down at her. "But that's ancient history. What we have to worry about now is the present. And I can't help but think that you would be better off if you hadn't chased that detective away."

"You think I really might need someone to guard me before this thing is over?"

"I don't know. I truly don't know. But it can't hurt, can it?"

"I'll think about it." Val glanced at her watch. She was already more than five minutes late. "But I'm sure even a practical joker as sick as this one wouldn't resort to murder."

"You're probably right," he said, "but there is one more thing to consider."

"What's that?"

"Has anyone told you *everything* that happened to Mrs. Forster before she was killed?"

Val frowned. "I thought I'd been told everything. But from the tone of your voice, I gather there's more?"

"Just one thing. Like you, Mrs. Forster had a cat. You know that the first threat was in the form of a note attached to the cat's collar."

"I know." A leaden feeling had begun to grow in Val's stomach as she waited for him to go on.

"The last threat—another note—was attached to the cat, too. But the cat was dead. It had been killed. They found it—Martin found it—in the alley behind the house. The note said, 'Your turn will come—soon.' That—killing the cat—was what finally made Sheriff Hyatt decide to post guards. For all the good they did!"

The leaden feeling had enveloped Val's entire midsection. She could feel her heart pounding.

"And you think," she said, her voice oddly flat, "that even if this joker doesn't have any intention of killing *me,* he might very easily kill Muldoon as part of the joke?"

Lawrence nodded uncomfortably, and Val couldn't find any reason to disagree.

Chapter 8

During her supper break, Val slipped into her poncho and went to the dime store a block from the library and bought a water pistol. At Wilt's Grocery two doors down on Main, she bought a bottle of the most concentrated ammonia solution she could find. It might not be as effective as a tear gas pen or Mace, but it was probably effective enough. And it was certainly more easily available, not to mention legal.

Then she detoured past the *Tribune* office and glanced in. It was deserted except for Katherine Roberts, who was standing over one of the desks, putting a note on top of one of the type-writers. She stood looking down at the note for a second and then, apparently satisfied, turned and started toward the door. She was shrugging into a light, half-length leather jacket when her eyes drifted toward the office-wide front window. Her square, almost masculine face softened into a smile and her pace quickened. As she closed the door behind her, she waved a greeting to Val.

"I've been meaning to call you," she said as she joined Val on the sidewalk. "But you know how that goes, one thing after another."

"I know," Val agreed, and glanced up at the clock in the courthouse tower across the street. "In fact, I have to get back pretty soon. We're expecting another avalanche of freshman science students this evening. The first wave was already in just after school. You wouldn't believe some of the questions old Jarvis hands out for 'research.'"

"Yes, I would. Don't forget, I've lived here most of my life. He was asking the same questions thirty years ago, and I haven't found the answers to some of them to this day. But what I wanted to talk to you about, Val, is your old friend, Edna."

"Mrs. Plover? What now?" Val had almost forgotten the woman in the rush of other events. "My bibliography again?"

Katherine grinned. "If you mean 'that list of perverted trash' that you gave Mrs. Wright and some of the other teachers, yes. I've never seen Edna so worked up. You must not have been suitably contrite at their meeting last night."

"I suppose not. I'm not much good at outright lying."

Katherine's grin faded. "I know how you feel. But—well, I had better warn you, it looks as if she's really going to go after you at the board meeting next week."

"Oh?"

"Two of her group phoned already today, 'critical letter to follow.' I suppose we'll have to run at least one of them. I wish I didn't have to, but . . ." She shrugged. "An unbiased press and all that."

"I understand," Val said. "Don't worry about it."

Katherine grinned again. "That was supposed to be my line. I was supposed to tell *you* not to worry."

"About Edna?" Val shook her head. "Believe me, Edna Plover is one of my lesser worries at the moment. In fact, one of my other worries is why I came by your office just now. I hoped I'd catch you in."

"Oh?" The older woman's eyebrows raised as she looked down at Val. "Would you care to tell me about it? I don't suppose it would have anything to do with that note someone put on your cat's collar a few days ago, would it?"

Val glanced at her, frowning. "How did you know about that?"

"A couple people, but I suspect the original source in both cases was Sarah Allen."

Val sighed. "Probably. I suppose the whole town knows about it now."

"Most probably, yes. Or a good percentage of it, at least. But don't worry, I have no intention of printing anything about it in the *Trib,* even if it would make a pretty interesting story."

"You have no idea *how* interesting," Val said, shaking her head. Hastily, she outlined the rest of the week's events. "Now this is definitely not for publication, mind you," she finished.

"Of course not," Katherine agreed. "In fact, I'd advise *you* not to tell anyone you don't absolutely have to. From what I know about practical jokers, all they really want is attention and reaction. Like obscene phone callers. Ignore them and it takes the fun out of it for them. Actually, that's the main reason—aside from concern for Martin Forster, of course—that I haven't run anything about it. I don't want to encourage the creep."

"I hope you're right," Val said. "And I thank you for not printing anything. But the reason I came by, I'm afraid, is to ask you yet another favor."

"Anything. Well, *almost* anything. What is it?"

Hurriedly, Val told her what Sheriff Lawrence had said about Sandra's cat and her own. "So what I need is a safe place to leave Muldoon for a while. Do you think he could coexist with your Willis?"

Katherine took Val's hand. "Of course. From what I've seen, Muldoon could coexist with almost anyone or anything. And I'd be glad to take him for a few days. Sharon's always after me to let her get another one anyway." She laughed. "And one more litter pan in the basement isn't going to make that much difference."

With the arrangements for Muldoon made, Val hurried back to the library, feeling considerably better than when she had left little more than a half hour before.

Leaving her Gremlin parked at the curb in front of the house, Val paused by the walkway to tear off a dozen blades of grass, and then hurried into the house. Muldoon came sonaring in from the kitchen before she had the door closed and followed her to the couch, where she dropped her purse and satchel full of books and then herself. Muldoon was next to her in a second, pulling his bulldogged calf routine in hopes of getting his stomach scratched.

"Hasn't anyone ever told you that you're a cat, not a dog?" she muttered as she reached down and ruffled the fur under his chin.

Then, as she held the grass for him with the other hand, he rolled over and began to munch on it. Frowning, she came across a small matt in the hair beneath his neck. She shook her head and, as he finished the grass, she got the metal comb from the coffee table and began trying to comb out the matted hair. "How do you do it, cat?" she said, half under her breath. "You haven't been outside for days, and still you manage. You think you're going to get a merit badge for knot-tying your hair or something?"

Finally, after feeding him, Val got the cat carrier from the basement. She was about to hoist Muldoon into it when the doorbell rang.

It was Dan, "Just checking."

She told him about her session with Thelma. He pursed his lips in a silent whistle when she finished.

"No wonder Marty didn't want to talk to her," he said. "But hasn't Lawrence or anyone been able to convince her that Marty's about the only guy in town who couldn't possibly have done it?"

Val shrugged. "To a true believer, logic doesn't count. I suppose Martin's lucky she hasn't gotten her accusations printed in the paper. I gather she tells anyone who'll listen. I'm surprised you hadn't heard about it yourself."

"Probably because I never met the woman. And since Marty and I work together, a lot of people figure we're close friends or something, so maybe they're hesitant about telling me what they hear."

"Like the wife being the last to know about her husband's affair?"

"Something like that," he said, chuckling.

After a few minutes more of idle speculation, Val glanced at her watch. "I don't mean to rush you off," she said, "but I have an errand to run."

"Anything I can help you with?"

She shook her head. "No, I'm just—"

She stopped abruptly. There was no point in telling Dan—or anyone else—that she was taking Muldoon to Katherine's house. The fewer who knew, the safer he would be.

"Yes?" Dan prompted. "You're just what?"

She started to try to make up a reasonable sounding errand, but by the time she had thought of one, she realized that she wouldn't be able to tell Dan without making him suspicious. Whenever she tried to lie—or even mislead someone—her voice gave her away instantly, like Pinocchio's nose.

And then, angry at herself, she thought, My God, if I can't trust Dan, I might as well give up.

"I'm taking Muldoon over to stay with Katherine Roberts and her family for a few days. I just found out what happened to Sandra's cat."

He frowned puzzledly for a second, but then his face cleared. "Oh, yes, I remember." He grimaced. "A nasty business. You think whoever's doing these things might kill Muldoon as part of the 'joke'?"

"It's possible." She didn't tell him about the water gun and the ammonia, still in a sack in the car. Muldoon, apparently realizing it was supper time or later, had started pacing about the hallway, sonaring loudly while making a series of hopeful moves toward the kitchen.

"Maybe I *can* help," Dan said, reaching into his pocket. "I could drive you over there while you take care of the cat. That way you wouldn't have to put him in a cage or worry about—"

By the time Val realized what Dan was doing—taking his keys from his pocket—it was too late. At the first metallic rattle of the keys on their ring, Muldoon was gone, streaking down the hallway and out of sight. His tail, now drooping low, trailed behind him like a hairy cape.

Dan didn't notice the animal's disappearance. All he saw was Val's sudden lunge to grab his keys and smother the sound they were making. He looked at her in confusion as she released his hand.

"I always like to hold hands," he said, "but I got the distinct impression that that wasn't inspired by a sudden burst of affection."

"It wasn't. Now just put those things away, quietly, and whatever you do, don't jangle them—or anything else!—until the cat is safely transferred."

As quietly as he could, he slipped the keys into his pocket. "What's going on? I get the feeling I just missed an entire scene change."

"I'm sorry. I didn't mean—" She shook her head. "It's just one of Muldoon's idiosyncrasies. For some reason, rattling car keys are the only things—the only things I know of, at least—that send him running for cover."

"Why in the world is that?"

"Who knows? It was probably that fifty-mile trip to my place when I first got him. The people that owned him before brought him down in a car, and he was absolutely frantic by the time it was over. And he's had a couple trips to the vet to be boarded for a few days. But whatever it is, rattling car keys really set him off. I suppose he figures he's in for another disastrous trip or something."

She glanced around, listening. "You're the one that caused the problem, Daniel," she said. "You can at least give me a hand finding him."

"What about that noisy can full of his food? I thought that hauled him in pretty fast."

"Under normal circumstances, yes, but not after car keys. Now come on, you take the kitchen, I'll try the bedroom."

Val finally found him under her desk in the office and managed to haul him out and drop him into the carrier. Being careful to muffle his keys at all times, Dan drove them to the Roberts' house about four blocks south.

Muldoon, once the carrier was opened in the Roberts' living room, however, seemed perfectly calm once again, as if nothing had happened. He hopped out of the carrier and began a patrol of the entire house, interrupted only by a brief meeting under the kitchen table with Willis, the Roberts' tan-and-white short-hair who, after the meeting, trooped along in Muldoon's wake, warily reinspecting every nook and cranny that Muldoon sniffed at.

Dan, meanwhile, brought in the newly cleaned and empty litter pan along with a fresh bag of cat litter. Sprague, Katherine's salt-and-pepper crewcut husband, guided Dan to the basement, where Willis's pan was kept. Sharon, the fifteen-year-old daughter, all long blond hair and glasses, followed Muldoon on his exploratory tour, interrupting him occasionally to give him a reassuring stroking. He was obviously making himself at home, and Sharon's only concern was, "How long can we keep him?"

It was after eleven when Dan and Val left, and it was after midnight when Dan climbed into his Checker and drove away from Val's.

It was just after one-thirty when the phone rang.

Startled, Val almost dropped the book she had been reading since going to bed an hour before. Then, as the purely physical reaction to the sudden noise faded, a chilling uneasiness gripped her. At this time of night, she thought as she carefully lay the book on the covers next to her and reached for the receiver, a telephone call can only be bad news. Something wrong with her mother? The last time Mother had gone in for her annual checkup, they had told her to lose thirty pounds, but there had been nothing seriously wrong.

But if it wasn't her mother . . .

Finally, she had the receiver in her hand and was holding it lightly to her ear.

"Hello?"

There was only silence, no dial tone, no breathing, nothing.

"Hello? Who is this?"

Then, as she was about to hang up, the voice began. It was a whisper, hoarse and muffled.

"You won't get away with it. If I can't have you, no one will."

"Who—"

"Did you think I would forget so soon, Sandra? That weekend in Cincinnati?"

A mixture of fear and anger flooded through Val as the voice whispered on, describing in graphic detail a sexual encounter, presumably between himself and Sandra, at some nameless motel. This was totally different from the note. That had been somehow impersonal, almost unreal, merely marks on a piece of paper, no matter what those marks said. But the voice on the phone drove home the fact that whoever had made those marks was *real*. He was out there in the night at this very instant, able to reach her at will, while she was powerless, unable even to imagine what he looked like.

But then, abruptly, her anger gained the upper hand, its heat driving out the chill that had blanketed her.

"In the first place," she broke in angrily, drowning out the whispered recitation, "I'm not Sandra! Now, if you're not too much of a coward, why don't you tell me who *you* are?"

The whispering voice faltered to a stop as Val's words overwhelmed it, but, as soon as she fell silent, it began again, repeating the words it had been speaking when she had interrupted. For whatever reason, this seemingly mechanical response encouraged her.

"You don't want to tell me?" she prodded, her own voice steady now, easily able to ride over the other's repeated attempts to continue. "All right, it doesn't matter whether you tell me or not. I know you're some sick-minded cretin who's out to play a stupid, cruel practical joke on Martin Forster! And that's all I *need* to know! You're not going to get anywhere this way! You can send me all the moronic notes you want! You can make all the idiotic phone calls you want, in the middle of the night or whenever the fancy strikes you! But Martin Forster will never know! From now on, I'm not playing your stupid game! I'm not telling Martin! Is that clear? He won't even know you exist, not from me!"

She listened for a second. The whisper had again faltered into silence, and this time it did not resume. She could hear the faint sound of labored breathing.

"You got the message, did you?" she asked. "It's not going to work!"

She listened to the distant breathing for another moment and then slammed the receiver into the cradle.

In the sudden silence, her own breathing was audible. And as she drew her hand back from the telephone, she saw that it was trembling.

For a long time he sat motionless, the lifeless receiver in his hand. Finally, unsteadily, he hung it up.

The darkness of the night beyond the windows seemed to be closing in, physically smothering him, as he forced himself to admit the truth:

She was right.

It would not *work! If Forster was not told, the entire plan would collapse.*

The endless waiting, the planning and the work—the perfume, the music, the pieces of jewelry, a dozen other things as yet undiscovered—would all be for nothing. The hope he had nurtured so carefully through the endless years would evaporate. Hope would be gone, as Sandra herself was gone.

And without hope—even for revenge, let alone redemption—there was no point to his existence. If he failed, he would prove himself to be no better than that spineless fool himself! And that was unthinkable.

There had to be a way!

Even now, there had to be a way . . .

Chapter 9

Val told Sheriff Lawrence about the call, and that he was the only one she planned to tell. He agreed it was a good idea to handle it that way, but, "if he continues to call anyway, you'd better let me see about getting a wiretap set up. Or at least a trace."

He looked surprised when she told him about the explicit and graphic language the caller had used.

"Odd," he said. "That note you got was identical to the original, right down to the type of printing. But this call— Are you sure you just didn't get an obscene phone call? You're sure it's part of the same thing?"

"Positive," she said, leaning back in the chair across from the desk in Lawrence's spartan office. "He called me Sandra, right at the start. And warned me again that I wasn't going to 'get away with it.'"

Lawrence frowned, biting his lip. "That part is the same as with Mrs. Forster. But the rest . . ." He shook his head. "That's something else, something else altogether."

"What sort of calls did *she* get?"

"I don't know the exact words, since none of them were recorded, but they weren't like what you just described. Un- less . . ." His voice trailed off as he leaned back in his chair and drummed his fingers on its bare metal arm. "Unless," he went on, "Mrs. Forster was censoring what the caller said. Con- sidering the fact that she was trying to cut herself off from her past as much as she could, and considering the change she had apparently undergone, I suppose she could have been reluctant to go into that kind of detail. Or even to use that kind of language. Look, I don't want to embarrass you, but exactly what was it he said?"

As she told him, his frown deepened. He interrupted after a few sentences. "It's the same incident described in Mrs. Forster's first call," he said. "It's just that this one is . . . unexpurgated, I guess you'd say. A lot more details."

"Didn't you tell me before—or maybe it was Dan—that whatever the caller said pointed to a particular ex-boyfriend?"

Lawrence nodded. "That's right. This one—the 'weekend in Cincinnati'—was Mike Moore. He and Mrs. Forster—Miss Haynes, I should say—had gone there, oh, at least a year before. No secret about it, at least not among Mike's friends. Or among hers."

"But it wasn't this Mike Moore who made the call?"

"Very unlikely. Mrs. Forster told us—very reluctantly—who the 'Cincinnati weekend' had been with, and we checked Moore out. He had an alibi for the time of the call. Besides, a couple of days later there was another call. This one was about a similar weekend in Indianapolis. Only this time it had been with Tommy Ailswurth. Again, the weekend had been no particular secret. Probably half the guys in town knew about it, including the motel they stayed at. And the details about what happened between them in the motel—well, they were too vague to prove or disprove anything."

Val brightened. "But this time, with a couple of the details he gave me . . ."

Lawrence sighed. "I'll check."

He phoned her at the library that afternoon with the results. "According to Moore, it doesn't check out."

"He and Sandra didn't do any of those things?"

"To quote him more or less directly, 'No way. Not that I wouldn't have liked to, but Sandy only went in for very standard activities.' "

"If there's another call, and if it's about—who did you say? Ailswurth?—do you want me to listen long enough to get some details for you to check?"

"No," he said, and for an instant his voice was sharp. "No, you were right in what you did last night. With someone like this, the less reaction you give them, the more likely he is to give up."

Val could detect the silent "I hope" in the sheriff's tone.

After a typically wearisome Saturday of grocery shopping, doing her laundry, and desperation house cleaning—vacuuming, dusting bookshelves, picking Muldoon's hair off most of the furniture—she was very ready for Dan to pick her up and head for dinner and the Theodore Bikel concert in South Bend.

By the time they returned, it was after midnight, and her mood was better than it had been all day. Bikel's songs and easy-going, anecdotal patter was easily as good as she remembered from the time she had seen him half a dozen years before in Milwaukee. And, most importantly, she had managed to almost completely forget about the joker for the evening.

But as she shrugged out of her poncho—this one black, for evening wear—the emptiness of the house, without Muldoon's familiar sonaring demands for attention and food, brought it all back. And as Dan left an hour later, they held each other just a little tighter, just a little longer, and Val was a little less flip than usual in avoiding his slightly less casual than usual proposal. One of these days, she found herself thinking as she watched him cross the street to the Checker, one of these days . . .

In bed a few minutes later, drifting lazily toward sleep, she wondered blurrily if she were just thinking of Dan as a cat-surrogate. After all, he and Muldoon did share a certain shaggy charm, speaking of which, she would have to visit Katherine's in the morning and see how the beast was doing. Most likely he was being spoiled even worse than he already was. Sharon was obviously as much of a cat freak as Val herself.

Somewhere amid the meandering thoughts of Dan and Muldoon and Katherine and Sharon, Val fell asleep.

A half hour later, she was jerked suddenly and violently awake by the jangling of the telephone. Still groggy and disoriented from the brief period of sleep, she flailed about, unwrapping herself from the tangled sheet and finally managing to get the phone to her ear.

The voice whispering from the receiver, however, jolted the world into icy clarity with a single syllable.

The first, muffled words were, as far as she could remember, identical to those that had started the first call, warning her that she couldn't "get away with it," that if he couldn't have her, nobody could.

And then he began another recitation of reminiscences, equally as graphic as the first. The "Indianapolis weekend," she assumed.

"I told you the first time," she snapped, easily overriding the whispering voice, "it's not going to work! You can just forget it!"

She started to slam the receiver down, but a sudden change in the caller's voice stopped her.

"Wait!" it pleaded tinnily, the receiver a good foot from her ear. "You don't understand!"

Something new? she wondered, hesitating. Then, slowly, she brought the receiver back to her ear. The voice had fallen silent again.

You're right," Val said, "I *don't* understand. How about telling me so I *can* understand? For a start, tell me why you're doing these vicious things to Martin?"

A tense silence, and then, "It is *necessary!* I mean him no harm!"

"He apparently doesn't see it that way. But *why* is it necessary?"

"Because he must be forced to see—" Abruptly the voice stopped. For a moment Val thought it was going to take up its recitation again, but it didn't. "You have to take my word for it," it said, and Val almost laughed at the desperate earnestness of the still-whispering voice.

"Well, I can't!" she snapped. "Why should I? Who are you, anyway?" And when there was no answer, "You don't *really* think I'm Sandra, do you?"

For several seconds there was no answer, and Val thought she could hear someone swallowing nervously. Finally the voice said, "It doesn't matter who you really are. All that matters is that you are here, and Forster—"

The voice cut itself off sharply, and when it didn't resume, Val said, "You *do* know that Sandra is dead, don't you? That she was killed five years ago?" There was no answer, and Val could feel her heart begin to pound as she formed the next, inevitable question.

"Are you the one who killed Sandra?"

"No!" The single syllable exploded in her ear, but it was followed only by more silence and, finally, a click as the phone went dead.

Again he sat alone in the darkness, his failure like a dead weight around his neck. Her face—Sandra's beautiful face—flickered in his mind's eye. She seemed to be calling to him, as she had that terrible night, but he could not answer.

He had failed her then, and he was failing her now! He was no better than that blind, sniveling coward, Forster! No better at all!

If only he could approach the man directly, as he did the others!

But he could not.

He could not confront Forster directly—not yet—or the entire plan would collapse on itself. For, in order to confront Forster directly, he would have to reveal the complete truth to him, and that was something Forster was not ready for, not yet.

Or—irrational hope flared through him—could he be selling Forster short?

The man was a weakling, that much was obvious. But he had finally seen the "resemblance." And, with no prompting from anyone, he had hired that detective.

Neither was an act of personal courage, God knows, but they were at least encouraging. He had even faced up to Winters that night, though he didn't really know why, and that, too, was encouraging.

And, even without this woman's cooperation, there were still things that could be done, things that might still turn the trick.

Or was he simply rationalizing? Was Forster as hopeless now as he had been then?

But it didn't matter.

Whether Forster could be counted on or not, he had to continue.

And if the work he had already done on Forster was not to be totally wasted, he would have to work fast, much faster than he had planned. The final act would have to be in a matter of days, not weeks. And there was that other one who needed further preparation. The first contact had been satisfactory, but it had been only preliminary. He had planned a gradual campaign, at least a half-dozen calls, but now he could not afford the time. He would have to be direct, far more direct than he liked at this stage, but there was no help for it, not if Forster was not to be completely written off. And he was not ready to do that, not yet.

He picked up the phone and slowly dialed the long-memorized number. In his mind he saw the sleepy eyes struggling open, saw the hand reach clumsily for the clock next to the bed, heard the mumbled curses as the phone continued to ring.

"Hello? Who is this?"

The voice, when it finally came, was still edged with sleep, as he had expected it to be.

"The night you killed Sandra Forster," he said, "you were wearing dark trousers—dark blue, I think—and a dark turtleneck sweater with a single pocket with a small emblem stitched into it. You weren't wearing a jacket. You had taken it off before you began to strangle her."

"Who—" the voice tried to interrupt, but he continued with his recitation, his voice flat and unemotional despite the emotions that tore at his stomach and throat.

"As you put your hands on her shoulders, she drew back, but then she tried to kiss you. I assume she was desperate at

that point, willing to try anything to distract you, to save her life. She tried to kick you, too, but you forced her to the floor. That was just inside the door of the living room, and it was there that you strangled her. She clawed at you, but all she was able to do was tear the pocket on your sweater."

He paused, waiting, but the other said nothing.

"I have told you this," he went on, "to convince you that I am telling the truth when I say I know—and can prove—that you murdered Sandra Forster."

Again he fell silent, waiting. Finally, in a hushed whisper, the other spoke, "What do you want?"

Sudden elation flooded through him, drowning the agony his recital had generated. He had not expected such swift capitulation.

"I want nothing new," he said, "nothing you have not already done. I merely want you to murder someone."

When, little more than a minute later, he hung up, he knew that at least that part of his plan would work. Now if only he could be equally sure of Forster . . .

Chapter 10

Val, more puzzled than frightened by the caller's departure from the script, nonetheless checked to be sure that the ammonia-filled water pistol, in the drawer of the small table next to the bed, was easy to locate and grasp, even without having to turn the lights on. However, once she managed to stifle—or simply grew tired of—all the mental turbulence the call had stirred up, she did manage to get a good night's sleep.

In the morning she called Sheriff Lawrence at his home. He was as puzzled as Val by the caller's behavior, but he insisted that no more time be wasted. He said he would give her a cassette recorder with a tiny, suction-cup microphone that she could attach to the receiver in a matter of seconds if another call came. He also said he would arrange with the telephone company to have all calls to her number traced.

The rest of the morning was taken up with a call from her mother—Sunday was another maximum discount day for long distance—and a visit to Muldoon which, at Katherine's insistence, was extended to include lunch. Aside from Muldoon—who was, indeed, being spoiled thoroughly by Sharon—they talked as much about the upcoming library board meeting and the probable crusade by Edna Plover as about anything else.

"One of the callers from her little group—Jessica Milton, I think—was making noises about retaining counsel, though she wasn't very specific about the reason," Katherine said at one point. "You don't suppose Martin would know, do you?"

Val shook her head. "I doubt it. Unless he's the lawyer they decided to retain, and I think he would've told me if he were. Anyway, I don't think he and his aunt are all that close. Martin may be, well, 'conservative' in a lot of ways, but he's certainly not as much a fanatic as she is."

Most of the afternoon—a dreary, almost-rainy one, better suited to indoor activities anyway—was spent catching up on *PW, Kirkus,* and *Library Journal* reviews and reading and reviewing a couple of books herself for the statewide reviewing service she'd gotten involved with a few weeks before. She would have to get the reviews finished and in the mail in the next couple of days if she was going to beat the deadline for the next issue.

Dan, of course, called, and she very nearly told him to come on over. The combination of dreary, gray weather, the empty house, and the very fact that it was Sunday almost overcame her determination to stick to her work, but she somehow resisted the temptation. Luckily for her weakening resolve, Dan seemed to accept her "I-have-to-get-caught-up" excuse without much argument, and with a faint sigh, she returned to her interrupted task of trying to capsulize the latest adventure of an Indianapolis-based private eye. It was above average for the genre, and it seemed a natural for any Indiana library, yet even the Hazleton library didn't have any of the earlier books in the series, only the latest, which Val herself had ordered a month before. She would have to see if the others were still in print or if the publisher, like most, had remaindered everything after a year or two. Unfortunately, the first of the series was almost ten years old, so the chances of finding it were slim unless there had been a recent paperback edition.

Not long after supper—a TV dinner while she watched a segment of "60 Minutes" on the music industry's version of vanity presses—her doorbell rang. Following her recently acquired habit of taking a look at the front steps through the living-room window before actually going to the door, she saw that it was Martin Forster.

Suppressing an uneasy frown, she went to the door. "Yes, Martin?"

He stood, stiffly uncomfortable, looking down at her. "May I come in?"

She glanced up and down the twilit street. "No detectives this time?"

His lips tightened as he shook his head. "No, but I wish there were. Now may I come in?"

Shrugging, she stepped back. "If you wish."

"Thank you." He nodded formally as he moved past her. She closed the door and followed him into the living room. He didn't seem to notice the untidy stacks of books on the coffee table in front of the couch or the half-dozen sheets of paper torn from her notebook on the arm of the couch.

"What can I do for you, Martin?" she asked when the silence had stretched on to at least thirty seconds with no end in sight.

"Has anything more happened?" he asked.

She managed a smile and an almost-laugh. "More bottles of rogue perfume, you mean? Or jewelry?"

His features, handsome enough in a darkly severe way, stiffened even more. His hands retreated to the pockets of his immaculately tailored, dark gray jacket. "I would have thought," he said, "that that incident would have caused you to treat the matter more seriously."

"And *I* thought we had agreed that the whole thing was just a bad-taste joke aimed at you, not me. Look, Martin, why are you here? If you're just checking to see how the joke is progressing, I've just told you—it isn't."

He swallowed audibly as he looked down at her. Then, turning his back on her, as if unable to continue as long as she was in his field of vision, he stood looking out the window at the fading light. His hands came out of his jacket pockets and clasped themselves behind his back, as if of their own volition.

"That's certainly a part of it," he said, "but there's more."

"And that 'more' is . . . ?" she prompted when he again fell silent.

"I know you will find it hard to believe, but— Will you hear me out? No matter how paranoid my ideas may sound?"

"Paranoid? About the joke? Look, thinking someone is playing a bad joke on you isn't paranoid, it's the truth."

"I know. I know that the engagement announcement and the other things were part of a tasteless joke. But recently I've begun considering even more disturbing possibilities."

"Such as?"

Still facing the window, he went on, slowly, "Do you remember that I pointed out your resemblance to Sandra?"

"Yes. But no one else sees that much of a similarity between us." She shrugged. "We're the same size and shape and general physical type, but that's all. No one else has noticed it." She didn't mention that, once the resemblance had been pointed out, both Dan and Katherine Roberts had agreed that it definitely existed.

"The resemblance is there," he said doggedly. "It's as real as that pin you found. And the perfume."

"All right, so there's a slight resemblance. I'll even go so far as to admit that it's possible that whoever's doing this also sees a resemblance and that it may even have jogged him into doing whatever it is he thinks he's doing. But I don't—"

"There may be more to it even than that," Martin said in a rush, turning suddenly to look at Val.

"What more could there be?"

He forced a faint smile onto the corners of his thin lips. "To a rational man, probably nothing. But to a paranoid like myself . . ." After a moment's silence, he plunged ahead. "Tell me, Val, how did you happen to come to Hazleton?"

She blinked at the sudden change. "I applied for the job at the library, and I was hired."

"I know that. But how did you come to apply?"

"I heard about the upcoming vacancy when Flora hit retirement age, so I applied."

"I know, I know. But I've talked to Mrs. Shoemaker. She told me that you wrote, asking about the job, before their ad appeared in *Library Journal*."

Val laughed. "There's nothing mysterious about that. Someone gave me a clipping of the article from the *Hazleton Tribune*."

"Who?"

"I don't know. The clipping showed up on my desk one morning, in an envelope with my name on it. The others *said* someone had dropped it through the book-return slot overnight, but I'm sure it was from one of the aides or librarians. I mean, there must've been fifty people in the system who knew the way I always griped about the nit-picking bureaucracy. I assume one of them stumbled across the item and sent it to me as a joke. Or as a hint."

"But did anyone ever admit doing it?"

"No. And I asked, believe me, especially after I got the job. I wanted to thank whoever it was, but no one ever owned up. But I don't see what *that* joke has to do with this one."

"I told you, it perhaps sounds paranoid, but I fear they might both be part of the same joke."

"What? How—"

"Whoever is doing this must have visited Milwaukee, and he must have seen you. And he must have seen the resemblance. Don't ask me how he knew you were dissatisfied and thinking about looking for another job. I don't know. Perhaps he didn't. Perhaps he simply took a chance. Perhaps he tried a dozen different women who resembled Sandra in a dozen different cities, and you're the only one who actually came to Hazleton."

"But *why?*"

"As the first step toward exactly what he's doing now!"

"You mean you think someone traveled all over the Midwest —or the whole country—looking for someone who vaguely resembled your wife, just on the off chance that she could be lured here to Hazleton to play this sick joke on you?" She snorted. "You were right. It *does* sound paranoid. Particularly when you're the only one who sees very much of a resemblance."

"I told you, I realize how it sounds. But the point is, it *is* possible."

She shrugged, trying to lighten the atmosphere. "I know. There's an old saying I read in a graffiti book once, 'Even paranoids have enemies.' "

He didn't smile. If anything, he looked grimmer. "And I obviously have an enemy. The only question is, how far will he go?"

"What you're suggesting is, *if* he's already gone to such lengths to get me to Hazleton, then he'll go to even greater lengths to carry out this bizarre practical joke on you? Lengths that might include actually killing me?"

He nodded stiffly, reluctantly. "Yes, I think it is entirely possible."

Val shuddered. "If you're trying to scare me, you're doing a bang-up job. But I still don't buy it. Look, now that you've had time to think about it, have you thought of anyone who might want to do this to you?"

"No, I can't imagine who it could be."

"What about Thelma, Sandra's sister?"

The color drained from his face. "You've spoken with her? About the pin?"

Val nodded. "She said it had been stolen. And she told me that you—"

"I know! I've heard it a hundred times, for God's sake! I *told* you there was no point in talking to her."

"That's why you didn't want anyone to talk to her?"

His breathing was shallow. He shook his head sharply, as if to clear everything away and start fresh. "None of that matters," he said. "The only thing that matters is your safety."

"I told you, I'm not worried," she insisted, with not quite total honesty.

"Very well, if you won't worry about yourself," he said, speaking rapidly, "will you worry about your cat?"

Coldness grabbed at her stomach. "What about him?"

"Do you know what happened to Sandra's cat? The cat I'd gotten her only a month before we were married? Has anyone told you *that?*"

"The sheriff told me. But there's nothing to worry about. Muldoon isn't here."

"What?" He glanced around sharply. "Where is he?"

"Someplace else. For safekeeping until this is over."

"Then you *do* take it seriously!"

"I'm just not taking any chances. Our joker friend might be a little quicker to kill a cat than he would a human."

"I wouldn't guarantee that. But where is he? Are you positive he's safe?"

"I'm reasonably sure. As sure as I can be, at least."

"But where? Are you boarding him somewhere?"

She shook her head. "The fewer people who know, the better."

He started to nod, as if in nervous agreement, but then he blinked again. He stood silently for a moment, a frown creasing his forehead, a frown that vanished as suddenly as it had come.

"You don't trust *me?*" There was a touch of sarcasm in his tone now, and his eyes narrowed in annoyance. "Are you forgetting that *I'm* the victim in this charade?"

"No, Martin, I'm not forgetting! Now please—"

"I suppose Richards knows!"

"As a matter of fact, he does. But he's the only one."

"He's keeping the cat himself?"

"No! Now listen, I don't care if I'm making sense or not, but I'm not telling you—or anyone else! I just do *not* want to take any more chances with Muldoon than absolutely necessary."

He was silent again, and as he watched her, the anger seemed to drain out of his face, out of his narrowed eyes. "Very well," he said, "if that's the way you want it."

"Come on, Martin, don't take it personally. I haven't even told the sheriff!"

"I'm not taking it personally. I fully understand." Then, as if out of nowhere, a faint smile appeared on his face, tilting the corners of his mouth, softening the hard lines of his jaw. "However, as long as I'm here, there *is* something I've been intending to ask."

Encouraged by his seeming shift in mood, Val returned the smile. "Yes? And what was that?"

"How did the tape Daniel made turn out? Is it available to be checked out of the library yet?"

She blinked. She had almost forgotten about the tape, which

Dan had turned over to her the evening of the fund raiser. "Not yet," she said. "It slipped my mind. But how did you know about it?"

"I was there when most of it was recorded, remember? And he's mentioned his donating it to the library to at least half the people who come through our offices."

"Oh?" She was both flattered and annoyed at Dan's apparent publicity campaign. "Luckily no one seems to have taken him seriously. At least no one has come into the library asking for it yet."

"Well? *I'm* asking for it. Do I get it?"

"It's not at the library yet. In fact, it's still around here somewhere."

"Then it shouldn't be all that much trouble, now should it? I'm really quite interested in hearing how it turned out."

Val grinned a little sheepishly. "I suppose I am, too. I haven't listened to any of it yet myself. Of course, once I do, I may not take it to the library at all, donation or no donation."

"So, why don't we both hear how it sounds? If one is to believe Dan, you could turn professional whenever you wanted."

"Dan has a big mouth and a tin ear, most likely," she said. "But if you're really interested . . . ?" And if it will keep you in a good humor and off the subject of our sadistic neighborhood joker, she added to herself.

"I am, very much."

"All right. But don't say I didn't warn you." She waved at the untidy couch as she started from the room. "Just make yourself at home. I'll see if I can dredge it up."

She walked down the darkened hall to her office and flipped on the overhead light. The clutter, largely because of her afternoon's effort to skim through and sort most of the magazines on the bookcase behind her desk, didn't leap out at her as much as it usually did. There was still the box of unpaid bills—utilities, book clubs, subscriptions, and God knows what else—and the box of clippings—movie and book reviews, recipes, store coupons, and general odds and ends—and a row of books from the library, but compared to its usual state, the tiny room was well organized. For one thing, Muldoon hadn't been around to jump up and bat small items to the floor, which was one of the tricks he tried occasionally when his sonaring and head-butting didn't get the desired results.

It took only a minute or two to paw through the desk and locate the tape, in the lower left hand drawer where she had presumably tossed it for safekeeping when she had gotten home that night.

Back in the living room, she dropped it into the cassette player she kept hooked up to her stereo, a modestly sized unit perched on top of a waist-high glass-fronted bookcase next to the TV set along the south wall of the room. During her brief absence, Martin had turned to the window again and was staring out into the almost total darkness—or perhaps at his own reflection, or at nothing at all. He didn't seem to notice her return.

There was a slight hum as she turned the stereo on, then a raucous crackling as she switched from the turntable input to the tape input. "I hope you don't want to hear the whole thing," she said, poising her finger over the cassette's "Play" button.

Martin twitched into life at the sound of her voice. He turned toward her jerkily. The subdued smile of a few minutes before was gone, replaced by a puzzled frown.

"The whole thing?"

"The whole tape. I mean, according to Dan, both sides are almost full, which means pretty close to ninety minutes. And I assume you heard most of it—in better fidelity—when he was recording it at the party."

"Oh. The tape. Yes, I suppose I did."

"Just a sample, then?"

He nodded, but the smile was still conspicuously absent.

She pressed the button and reached for the volume control on the cassette, turning it almost completely off, and then raising the volume on the record player.

After a few seconds, the first chords of a guitar came from the speakers. The sound was thinner and tinnier than she re-

membered from the brief sample Dan had played for her in the
car before the party. But maybe it was the acoustics, she told
herself. In the smaller enclosed space of the car, it just sounded
fuller.

"Guess it didn't turn out as well as I thought," she said,
shrugging. "Maybe I really *won't* take it in to the library. I
wouldn't want to prejudice the—"

Abruptly she stopped speaking as a voice joined the guitar. It
was a thin, reedy soprano, not unlike an amateur Jean Ritchie.

For an instant she wondered if the tape were running at the
wrong speed. She wasn't that familiar with her own voice, but
she knew it was at least an octave or two lower than the one
she heard now. A high contralto at best, certainly not a soprano.

A sudden chill rippled along her spine. Her hand darted out
and hit the "Stop" button and then jabbed at "Eject." The door
of the player popped open, the clacking sound loud in the sudden silence.

She snatched the tape from the player and held it up to the
light.

It was the same. Dan's laborious printing filled the minuscule
labels on both sides. "Valerie Hamilton," it said, and then, on
the second line in each case, "Misc. Folk and Fun."

"I don't understand," she said softly, disbelievingly. "It's the
same tape, but that can't be me singing."

"I know," Martin said softly. He was standing in the middle
of the room, his face starkly expressionless. "I know. That was
my wife. That was Sandra."

Chapter 11

For a moment that seemed to stretch on forever, Val stood frozen, Sandra's name echoing through her mind. Then, as the name faded, a chilling mixture of anger and fear spread through her. Everything else—the note, the pin, even the calls—had been to some extent impersonal. They had been directed at Martin, not at her. But this, the wiping out of her own voice and the substitution of another—that of a woman five years dead—suddenly broke through the shell she had erected around herself.

Suddenly it was totally personal—and frightening.

Whoever was doing these things, whether he meant harm to Martin or not, was, in his own warped way, doing more than simply trying to recreate what had happened five years before. He was, she realized, trying to recreate Sandra herself! By sympathetic magic or some such voodoo insanity, he was trying to make Val *become* Sandra!

Just as, on the tape, Val's voice had somehow become Sandra's.

And she thought: Could Martin be right? Could I have been tricked into coming to Hazleton, simply because I looked a little like Sandra? And could the person doing this be the same one who had killed Sandra?

And what happens when, in his twisted mind, I finally do become Sandra?

What will he do then?

His emotions were a boiling mixture of hope and frustration as he watched Forster leave the woman's house. It was obvious that Sandra's voice on the tape had had even more of an effect on him than he had hoped.

But even so, it would not be enough. Of that he was certain.

And still she refused to tell Forster of the calls. Even the shock of Sandra's voice on the tape had not been enough to make her blurt out the truth to him.

There had to be more. If the plan were to have even a remote chance of succeeding, there had to be more. Forster had to be subjected to more pressure.

If only the cat had not been taken out of his reach, that might well be enough. But it had been, and it appeared that there was no way of finding out where it had been taken.

He glanced back at the house, wondering, but he decided instantly that trying to listen at one of the windows would be not only fruitless but dangerous, especially now. She was probably already calling the sheriff. For him to lurk in the shadows, hoping vainly for a scrap of information to filter through the glass, would be foolish and pointless.

No, there had to be another way, either to find out where she had taken the cat—or to insure Forster's actions when the critical time came.

There had to be a way.

He could not give up now, not when success was so near . . .

Val couldn't raise either Dan or Sheriff Lawrence on the phone. There was no answer at Dan's number, and Mrs. Lawrence said her husband was out somewhere on unspecified departmental business. Grudgingly, she agreed to have him call Val when he returned, which she expected him to do momentarily.

Katherine Roberts, however, answered on the first ring.

"Val? There's nothing wrong, is there?"

"Martin was here," she said, and quickly outlined their discovery of the altered tape.

Katherine stopped just short of a gasp. "Then there's no question about it, is there? This person *has* been inside your house."

"It certainly looks that way. And it has to have happened in the last few days, since Dan gave me that tape."

"Have you told Mel?"

"I haven't been able to reach him yet. But I will."

"Perhaps you should reconsider Martin's offer of a body-guard," Katherine said.

"I'm thinking about it. In the meantime, I'm still keeping both doors chained."

"Do you have anything to protect yourself? If you don't—"

"A water pistol with ammonia. From what I've heard, that's as effective as anything."

"It is," Katherine said, "provided the solution is strong enough."

"You sound as if you've had experience with it."

"No, but a friend of mine in Atlanta has. She's convinced it saved her from being raped. But you have to be careful with it."

"I know. Not right in the face. The chest is close enough, and that way it won't do permanent damage and get you sued."

"Yes, but what I meant was, you have to be ready to get away from it yourself or the fumes will get you, too."

"Squirt and run?"

Katherine laughed. "That's about it."

"Thanks for the warning. But the real reason I called is Muldoon."

"You don't want him back, do you? Not after—"

"No, nothing like that. I guess I just wanted to keep you informed. Or 'warned,' I suppose I should say. If this joker can get into my house, there's no reason he can't get into yours."

"Don't worry about it. Besides, I didn't think you had let anyone know where he was."

"I haven't. I haven't even told the sheriff. But if whoever it is has been lurking around . . ."

"He might have seen you when you and Dan brought him over? Or when you visited today?"

"It's possible. And I wouldn't want to put you in any kind of danger."

"I told you, don't worry."

But as Val hung up a few minutes later, she couldn't help herself. On the other hand, she couldn't bring herself to insist on bringing Muldoon back here. Or taking him to a vet for boarding, where, with no one on duty at night, breaking in would be relatively easy. She could only hope that his whereabouts were unknown to the joker. Or that the joker wasn't as sadistic as she was afraid he might be.

She was reaching for the phone to try Dan again when it rang. The sheriff? she wondered as she snatched up the receiver.

"Hello?"

"Miss Hamilton?"

"That's right. Sheriff Lawrence?"

"No, I'm sorry. If you're waiting for a call, I'll—"

"No, that's all right. But who is this?"

"Earl Winters. You remember, last week? When your car stalled?"

"Of course. How are you?"

"Fine. And you? Or more to the point, your car? You said you were thinking of bringing it in for a tune-up."

She laughed. A Sunday night sales pitch? "It's been doing quite well, thank you. But you're right, I did say something like that, didn't I? Incidentally, the only people I've asked gave your shop a clean bill of health. So I probably will— Look, I get paid again the end of the week. If your bill won't be too outrageous, I might be able to handle it then."

"I can't guarantee anything—except your satisfaction. We always try to do that. You want to bring it in this week, then?"

"Might as well. Say Friday?"

"Perfect. And if you think the bill *is* outrageous, we can negotiate, most likely. Or you can take a while to pay. We're pretty informal around here. I'll even drop you off at the library when you leave the car, if you like."

"I might take you up on that. Where's your shop located?"

He gave her an address that sounded like the northeast edge of town.

"Unless I get a better offer," she said, "I'll take you up on that ride. It sounds like a fair distance from downtown."

"A mile or a little more. And I'll be glad to drive you. And pick you up in the evening."

"Do you offer this much personal service to all your customers?"

A brief hesitation, and then, "Just to pretty librarians being harassed by practical jokers. Which reminds me—have you had any more problems along those lines?"

"Why do you ask?"

"Sorry. I suppose it's none of my business, but I've been thinking. About the way your car stalled last week."

"Yes? What about it?"

"I don't want to scare you—or did I say that before? Anyway, like I said, I've been thinking about that. And there's a chance—just a small one, but a chance anyway—that somebody had been messing with your car. With the choke."

Suddenly the chill was back, and she tried to remember if she had fastened the chain on the front door when Martin had left.

"Why do you think that?" she asked, her voice unnaturally calm.

"Just a hunch, that's all. I mean, it was the sort of thing that someone *could* have done, in just a minute or two, probably. And you mentioned the practical jokes and all . . ." Winters' voice trailed off, as if he were embarrassed at the lack of logic in his explanation.

"Could you tell for sure if you looked at my car again?" she asked.

"I doubt it. I mean, the thing could've just worked loose by itself, or someone could've loosened it on purpose. There's no way of telling." Another hesitation, and then, "You sound like you think I might be right."

"Maybe," she said, as noncommittally as she could manage, but apparently she wasn't all that successful.

"Something else *has* happened," he accused. "Hasn't it?"

"What could've happened?" she persisted, knowing it was useless.

"You could've gotten some phone calls, just the way Sandra Haynes—Sandra Forster, I mean—just the way she did. Have you?"

"What if I have?"

"For God's sake, Miss Hamilton! I'm just trying to help! Can't you see that?"

Val was silent a moment, feeling both annoyance at his persistence and guilt at her own reluctance to trust him.

"All right," she admitted, "I did get a couple of calls."

"I thought so. Were they the same kind Mrs. Forster got?"

"Similar."

"But . . . ?" he prompted.

"But more explicit."

A short silence, as if Winters were trying to digest that bit of information. Then he asked, "Do you have any idea why these things are being done to you? Any idea at all? Did the calls themselves give you any idea?"

"It's obviously a practical joke of some kind."

"On you?"

"On Martin Forster, I assume. There's someone out there with something against him, that's all. Sort of like recreating Ford's Theater for Mrs. Lincoln."

"You're sure it's a joke on Martin? Couldn't it be on you? Maybe you've made an enemy or something? Maybe the whole 'joke' angle is just a cover-up of some sort."

"Cover-up for what? I've made some enemies, but I don't really think Edna Plover would go in for that kind of retaliation."

"Edna Plover?"

"It's a long story," she said, and told him as briefly as she could about her trouble with Edna Plover and her group. "Anyway," Val finished, "she's not a candidate for the caller. From the voice, I'm pretty sure it was a man. And as long as you're on the phone, would you care to whisper hoarsely at me?"

"I beg your pardon?"

"Since you're so interested in the joker, maybe you're him.

Whisper something—like Sandra's name, maybe—so I can compare your voices."

"You're taking this whole thing pretty lightly," Winters said irritably.

"Don't you believe it. I'm taking it more seriously all the time. And if *you* have any ideas as to who might be behind this idiocy, you let me know. Do you know anyone who hates Martin enough to do something like this to him?"

She could hear Winters pull in his breath, as if preparing for another protest, but then he said, in a subdued voice, "What about Sandra's sister? I've heard that she thinks Martin killed Sandra himself."

"I've heard the same thing, directly from her. But the caller's a man—or at least I think it is. Anyone else you can think of? Anyone at all?"

"No one. But I still think— Look, can you be absolutely sure that Martin is the one this stuff is aimed at? Are you sure it's not aimed at you yourself? I mean, after all, *you're* the one who's been getting the threats, not him!"

Then, abruptly, one short sentence the caller had whispered leaped into her mind, overshadowing all the others: "I mean him no harm."

They had been speaking of Martin Forster, and the caller had said, "I mean *him* no harm."

He hadn't, Val realized, said anything at all about not meaning *her* any harm.

Chapter 12

By the time Val finished talking to Earl Winters, Sheriff Lawrence was on her doorstep. He had tried calling, he said, but the line had been busy, and he had rushed over, bringing with him the cassette with the suction-cup microphone, which is what he had been out running down when she had called before.

"Was it number three?" he wanted to know immediately.

"No, it was just Earl Winters," she said, and explained the situation as well as she could.

"He's right, you know," Lawrence said. "You *are* the one who's been getting the threats. And I don't care what the budget committee says, one more threat and I'm putting a twenty-four-hour guard on you. And tonight I'll have Harry cruise by every half hour or so."

Then, when she told him about the tape, his scowl deepened even more. "I'll make that every *quarter* hour," he said. "And you—you be *very* sure you fasten the chains on your doors."

"Don't worry. I've been using them the last couple of days, and I don't intend to stop now." She didn't volunteer any information about the ammonia and the water pistol.

He looked at the tape uncomfortably where it lay next to the cassette. "I suppose you and Forster managed to destroy any prints there might've been on it."

She agreed that they probably had, but he took it with him anyway, careful not to damage any prints that might have survived. When she told him she hadn't been able to get hold of Dan yet, he said, "Don't. Not until I have a chance to talk to him, anyway."

She frowned. "What are you going to do?"

"I'm not sure. See how he reacts to the tape, at least."

"You don't think *he* has anything to do with it, do you?"

Lawrence shrugged. "He's the one who recorded it in the first place, don't forget. In any event, I'm not ruling out *anyone* —except myself, and I wouldn't blame *you* for not even doing that."

So she didn't tell Dan. She didn't even try calling him any more that evening, because she knew that he, like Earl Winters, would instantly see through her. It was only by sheer luck—or politeness on Dan's part—that she had so far been able to avoid telling him about the first phone call. And she hadn't talked to him since the second, except to keep him from coming over that afternoon.

In the morning, someone from the telephone company called her at the library to verify the sheriff's request for a trace on all incoming calls. "It's all done automatically," the woman explained. "You don't have to notify us about each call, nor do you have to hold the party on the line for a long period of time. Our computer will handle the entire operation and will give us a printout of the time and the originating number of each call."

A good part of the rest of the day was spent getting the month's statistics organized for presentation to the library board that evening—and trying to figure out the safest approach to take with Edna Plover and her legions. According to Katherine, they would be out in strength and looking for blood, preferably Val's. Not that they could draw any great amount, not immediately, but if Val responded the wrong way—with the anger she really felt or the sarcasm she thought they deserved—it could easily work against her. A harsh word or a cheap laugh at their expense might be momentarily satisfying, but such tactics—or lack thereof—could only gain Edna Plover a few sympathy votes, which was one of the last things Val wanted to do.

On the other hand, she couldn't act as if she were simply ignoring them; as if they weren't worth the trouble to oppose. That could be equally disastrous in the long run. Even Edna Plover's group, though farther out in right field than any other group Val personally knew of, was not *so* far out that it could be simply dismissed as foolish or unimportant. Too many purges of "objectionable material"—from *Tarzan of the Apes* to *Catcher in the Rye*—had started from equally "laughable" beginnings.

In midafternoon, however, her mind was yanked back to other matters. Apparently the sheriff had indeed gotten in touch with Dan Richards and, without any prelude or warning, had played the mysteriously altered tape for him. Dan, after the initial surprise wore off, had confirmed the fact that it was indeed his own handwriting still on the tape. Then, ignoring the senior partner's scowl, he had dashed out of their commune of offices to find Val and to demand to know why he hadn't been told about either the tape or the calls.

She pacified him as best she could with her explanation— "The less attention we pay to a practical joker, the less likely he is to keep on playing the joke." But he was still upset when he left.

"If this goes on much longer," he said in a parting warning, "*I'm* going to hire a bodyguard for you, whether you like it or not!"

"And I might just take him," Val muttered to herself as she returned to her belated preparations for the evening.

Like most of the meeting rooms in the Hazleton Civic Center, the one the library board held its meetings in was a converted classroom. Even the blackboard—or greenboard, if you wanted to be completely accurate—stretched clean and chalkless across the wall at the front of the room.

The three members of the board, Katherine Roberts in the center, sat behind a long, wooden table, their backs to the blackboard, glasses of water and notepads in front of them. Katherine, her square, lined face purposely neutral beneath the short, gray bangs, looked out over the half-filled room, her fingers resting lightly on the round metal paperweight she habitually used as a gavel. The men on either side of her—bald and roundish Cecil Walters and lantern-jawed, graying Harvey

Alber—nervously doodled on their notepads. They probably weren't used to this large a turnout, Val thought as she stood in the door at the back of the room. After Edna Plover's vitriolic "press release" had appeared in the afternoon's *Tribune,* though, they should have expected a fair-sized crowd. Val only hoped that the majority of them were appalled rather than approving.

As for Edna Plover herself, she and a half dozen of her followers occupied the front row of chairs like a battle line. Val recognized most of them from the meeting the week before. Scattered about the rest of the room were another fifteen or twenty people, most of whom she recognized as regular patrons of the library, even though she couldn't put a name to more than a couple. Near the end of one row not far from the door, Sharon, Katherine's daughter, looked back and waved as she saw Val.

Val returned the wave and moved along the side of the room toward the girl, glancing at the back of the room as she did. There were two men in the back row, several seats apart. One was Pete Driscol, a spry octogenarian who came in every Monday like clockwork for seven books, one for each day of the following week. Val was waving a greeting at Driscol when she belatedly recognized the other man a half-dozen seats away: Earl Winters. He smiled and shrugged, as if to indicate he didn't really know what he was doing here.

Then, as Val lowered her conservatively pant-suited form onto the chair next to Sharon's faded jeans, Katherine stood up and walked around the table toward Val. Edna Plover's narrowed eyes, peering out through the filmy, anachronistic veil that hung from her flowered hat, followed the board president's movements disapprovingly.

Katherine made a brief pass at smoothing her gray skirt as she dropped sideways onto the vacant chair directly in front of Val. She leaned across the back of the chair and whispered, "You've seen the army in the front row, I assume."

Val nodded. "They're really out in force. And there's no need to say 'I told you so.'"

Katherine grimaced and leaned closer. "As I've repeatedly told you, I don't think you have anything to worry about, but it does look more and more as if Edna—or one of her lieutenants —is going to make a formal request for your dismissal this evening. Using that 'reluctant readers' bibliography of yours as the basis for the request."

"Has she talked to you about any of this?"

"Not personally, but a couple of her army stopped me in the hall to chat. Anyway, I just wanted you to be prepared for the worst."

"Thanks. I appreciate it. But I've got a couple of friends of my own, I notice," Val said, nodding toward the two men in the back row. "Besides," she added, grinning, "I've been preparing most of the day, trying to figure out a diplomatic way of turning the other cheek while not giving an inch."

"You're starting to sound like a politician," Katherine said, returning the smile.

"Thanks again, I think." Val glanced at the front row. "If looks are any indication, she may call for *your* resignation, too. I think she's trying to stare a hole in your back."

"If all she does is stare, I don't worry. Incidentally, have you found out what happened to that tape of yours yet?"

"Nothing new. Someone got it and recorded Sandra's voice over mine." Val shivered. "As I told you last night, I'm keeping the doors chained and the ammonia pistol handy."

"I don't blame you. But Sprague and I have been talking about this whole thing, and we were both wondering if you would like to stay with us for a while?"

"Would you?" Sharon spoke up suddenly, her hand touching Val's jacket sleeve. "We've got an extra room that never gets used now that Hal's away at college." Hal Roberts was Sharon's older brother, currently a freshman at Purdue in Lafayette.

Automatically, Val shook her head despite the warm feeling that the invitation, particularly Sharon's spontaneous endorsement, gave her. "No, thanks. I'll be all right. For one thing, the phone company's got their computer set up to trace all the calls

I get, so if this character calls once more, we'll know who he is."

"If he calls from where he lives," Sharon said promptly.

Val grimaced. "Yes, there is that possibility. But even if he calls from a pay phone, it'll be a start. There aren't that many around Hazleton. Not like Milwaukee or somewhere where there are as many pay phones as there are families in Hazleton. Besides, the sheriff is threatening to give me a bodyguard if I get any more calls and they still can't run the guy down. No, I'll be all right. I'm not saying I'm not a wee bit tense, but I'm sure it will work out. Besides, you've already got one house guest. Speaking of which, how's he doing?"

Katherine, whose face had taken on a solemn look as she issued the invitation, found a smile. She stood up. "You and my daughter can discuss the cat situation. She's the one he follows around all the time." Briskly, she made her way back to the table at the front of the room.

"Is that true?" Val asked the girl.

"Pretty much. Last night he slept on my feet, I think." She laughed. "At least there was a warm, hairy spot on the blanket down there when I woke up this morning. And he was sitting in the doorway staring at me."

"I gather he's fitting right into the household, then."

"Of course." Then Sharon's face grew serious. "But I do think he misses you."

"Sure he does," Val said. "You're just anthropomorphizing. One warm body that provides food and petting is as good as any other."

Sharon shook her head. "I really think he misses you. I really do."

"And who might that be?" A masculine voice came from a few inches behind Val. Jerking around in her seat, she saw a faintly smiling Martin Forster seated in the chair immediately behind her.

"Just Muldoon, Mr. Forster," Sharon said. "We've been—" She broke off as she belatedly noticed Val's sudden frown in her direction.

"You've been keeping him for a couple of days for Miss Hamilton, right?" Martin finished for her.

When Sharon remained uncomfortably silent, glancing at Val out of the corner of her eye, Val sighed. "That's right, Martin. That's the secret hideout. Just don't tell anyone, that's all I ask."

His faint smile faded into solemnity. "Don't worry," he said, "I won't. I remember what happened to—" He stopped, a frown creasing his brow. Then he shook his head. "Don't worry," he repeated, "I won't tell anyone."

"What are you doing in here, Martin?" Val asked. "I thought your zoning board meeting was being held down the hall this evening. Aren't you supposed to be down there holding Lichtenwalter's hand? He did get back in town, didn't he?"

"He did," he said, "but Dan is taking care of it for me."

"But you've been working with the man all through this shopping center thing, haven't you?"

"The zoning board is just routine," he said. Then, before she could rephrase her question or try another one, he leaned close, glancing sideways at Sharon, who was still looking at him. His lips close to Val's ear, he whispered, "Could I talk to you for a minute?" With his eyes and a minuscule nod, he indicated the door to the hall at the rear of the room.

Frowning, Val glanced at her watch. Still five minutes until the meeting officially started. She nodded. "Be back in a minute," she said, touching Sharon's arm. "Save my seat."

Martin was waiting in the ill-lit hall as Val emerged from the meeting room. "What now?" There was a touch of annoyance in her voice as she remembered the last time he had taken her aside like this. That time it had been to tell her she looked like Sandra. And then last night . . .

"I've been doing a lot of thinking since last night," he said.

"So have I."

"I'm sure you have. The point is, I'm convinced that you can't be safe in your house anymore. It's obvious that whoever is doing these things has been inside it at least twice, once to take the tape and once to return it—unless you've been carrying it with you?"

She shivered slightly as she shook her head. "I put it in my desk that same evening. But I'll be all right. Besides, I think the whole thing is probably over. After all," she lied, "I haven't gotten any calls from whoever it is. And if you were right about this 'recreating Sandra' idea, then he would have called by now."

He stared down at her, a sudden look of anger pulling at his shadowed features.

"It doesn't matter," he said, "whether he calls or not. What matters is that you shouldn't take any chances. I know you lock and chain your doors at night, but chains can be broken. Locks can be picked. Windows can be forced or broken." He shook his head determinedly. "No, I've thought it through, and you simply cannot be safe by yourself in that house." His voice was hard despite the solicitousness of his words.

"Don't worry about it. I can take care of myself." She thought briefly of showing him the ammonia-filled water pistol in her purse, but decided it would only re-enforce his conviction that she was in danger.

She started to turn away, but he caught her arm. His grip was bruisingly tight. "You should move somewhere else," he said, "at least for a few days. It's the only sensible thing to do."

She frowned, not only at his grip but at his advice. "As you may have overheard just now, if you started eavesdropping soon enough, I've already turned down an invitation to stay with Katherine and her family. I'm certainly not going to move in with you."

He looked blank for a second before shaking his head and frowning. "I didn't mean anything like that, of course. I merely meant that I own a house that I normally rent out. It's currently vacant, and you could move in there for as long as necessary. Or as long as you like. Rent free, of course. This entire affair *is* my fault in a way, so the least I can do is try to keep you from being harmed."

"I understand that, Martin, and I appreciate it. But I told you, I'll be all right. And I really must be getting back inside."

His grip tightened on her arm rather than loosening. "I don't think you appreciate the seriousness of the situation," he said earnestly. "Whether this person has called you or not, he *is* still out there! To be perfectly honest, I find his *not* calling more ominous than if he *had* called. At least then we would have a schedule, a timetable to base our actions on. But this way—"

"Martin, please! There's no point in discussing it!" She was trying hard not to blurt out the truth about the calls. "Now I have to get inside. The meeting is starting."

"No! Not until you understand the seriousness of what you are facing!"

"We can talk about it later, Martin!"

"No! You have to see *now* what could—"

"Stop it, Martin! Look, I didn't want to tell you any of this, but if it's the only way to get you to let me go, I guess I'll have to. He *has* called, twice! He has told me—in great detail—about the Cincinnati weekend and the Indianapolis weekend!"

"When—"

"It doesn't matter when!" she snapped, rushing on. "The thing is, he *is* on schedule. And if he calls again, we'll have him. The phone company computer is set up to trace all calls to my phone, so all we need is one more call. So you see, there's nothing to worry about. We'll know who it is as soon as he calls again, and that will be that. Now will you let me go so I can get in to the meeting?"

His eyes had widened. "I didn't know." Then he blinked. "But I still feel you would be safer if you—"

"Well, *I don't!*"

With a sudden movement, she was able to jerk free of his loosened grip. She stood a yard from him, watching him warily. He seemed disoriented, and she wondered if, even considering the provocation he had given her, she should have blurted out what she had about the calls. He was, after all, as much a victim in all this as she herself.

"Are you all right?" she asked, her voice subdued now.

He blinked again and shook his head. He darted glances about the shadowy hall, a frown creasing his forehead deeply. He looked at Val.

"What was that?" he asked. "What were you saying?"

"I just asked if you were all right. Are you?"

"I—I think so," he said, but the frown remained.

I definitely shouldn't have told him, she thought. "I'm sorry," she said, "but you *were* getting a little rough." She could still feel where his fingers had dug into her arm.

His puzzled frown only grew deeper at her words. "I'm sorry," he said uncertainly. "I didn't mean to be."

"It's all right," she said hastily. From inside the meeting room, she could hear the cracking sound of Katherine's paper-weight gavel. "The meeting is starting. We can talk later if you want to."

He was nodding his agreement as she turned and hurried into the meeting room. Katherine was just asking Harvey Alber to read the minutes of the last meeting as Val slipped into her seat next to Sharon, who had been watching the door curiously.

The meeting went about as expected. After the minutes were read and accepted, Val gave her report on circulation and other activities and problems, including her already traditional request for a new—or at least newer—typewriter. She concluded with a few words on the success of the fund raiser for the cassette collection and announced that tapes had already been ordered but that most would probably not arrive for at least two or three weeks. When someone in the audience—someone Val remembered from the fund-raising party—asked about the tape Dan Richards had been making of Val's singing, she just said it hadn't turned out.

"Mechanical problems with the recorder," Katherine added when the questioner looked as if she were going to persist. "It didn't come out at all."

When Katherine opened the meeting for "remarks from the public," Edna Plover was, as expected, the first on her feet.

"Yes, Edna?" Katherine said. "You have something to say?"

"Indeed, yes." Mrs. Plover took two slow steps forward until she was standing at one end of the table, then turned so that she was facing the spectators as much as she was the three members of the board. For a moment her eyes rested on Val, then turned to Katherine and the two men at the table. Mrs. Plover's wine-red dress stood out against the green of the blackboard. Her row of followers waited expectantly.

"Some of you, I am certain, know the reason for my rising to speak at this time," she began. Her thin voice enunciated each word meticulously, and there was a faint trace of a New England accent even though she had been born and raised in Hazleton. "Some, too, are certainly aware of my position in regard to the Hazleton Public Library, indeed in regard to all public libraries. It is the same position that was held by those who, thousands of years ago, originated the concept of the library. They meant libraries to be repositories for the best books of the age, records of what the best minds of the day had to tell us. Libraries were meant to be a proud heritage, containing material of proven worth. Sadly, that noble concept is no longer fashionable. The concept now in vogue—and you will pardon me if I speak frankly—the modern concept seems to me to be nothing more than simple pandering!"

Val heard a sudden, hissing intake of breath next to her. "That woman!" Sharon whispered to Val in outrage. "You should sue!"

Val put a hand on the girl's arm. "Don't let it bother you," she whispered back, but from Sharon's expression, she was obviously unable to take Val's advice.

At the front of the room, Edna Plover continued to speak of pandering, comparing the bulk of the library's purchases to the junk food with which crassly commercial enterprises pandered to the degraded eating tastes of the current generation. Eventually, of course, she got around to Val's "reluctant readers" bibliography, waving it before the front row like a red flag and talking about "the ultimate junk food of the mind, the drugstore-rack paperback," which was liberally represented in the bibliography, and the "mentally nutritious fare, the classics that once were in favor but apparently are no more." She also discussed at length the resultant "starvation" of the reading public, which, she was certain, "deserved much better nourishment for their money."

Finally, though, she was finished, placing a copy of Val's bibliography in front of each board member as she asked formally for Val's dismissal. As she returned to her seat, there was polite applause from the front row and a couple of murmurs of approval from elsewhere.

Val, meanwhile, had been mentally rewriting all her remarks to take into account—to take advantage of—Edna Plover's junk-food-vs-nutritious-literature analogy. When Katherine gave Val the floor, she began with a listing of a few of the accepted classical authors who had, in their own times, been accused of writing trash—Shakespeare, Scott, Poe, etc. Mainly, however, she settled for pointing out that one of Mrs. Plover's basic assumptions was wrong. If all the "junk food literature" were taken away, she pointed out, people would not, as Mrs. Plover insisted, partake of a "more nutritious literary diet." More likely, they would simply starve. They wouldn't read anything at all.

"The choice," Val finished, "is not between junk food and filet mignon. It is between some food—*any* food—and no food at all. And the titles on my 'reluctant readers' bibliography are simply a few of those which, in my own experience and the experience of many other librarians and teachers, have a better-than-average chance of attracting the interest of those who, otherwise, would probably read nothing beyond the daily headlines and TV listings. And if they at least get into the habit of reading *something,* who knows where it will lead? Maybe even to a nutritious classic or two someday."

There wasn't any applause as Val sat down, but there were a number of understanding nods and murmurs, including, she was surprised to note, one from a woman in the front row, only two seats away from Mrs. Plover. A couple of the nodders even

got up to second what Val had said, and one—Harriet Carlson—
said that her son, Gary, had read one of the books on Val's list,
and it was the first thing other than class assignments he had
read in the last three years. "Sure, it was based on characters
from some TV series, but at least he was reading about them
instead of just staring at the tube." And from the back row,
Pete Driscol, his voice remarkably clear and steady for someone in his eighties, stood up to ask if he could get a copy of the
list himself. "I got a couple of grandkids that act like you asked
'em to take castor oil if you try to get 'em to read something."

When the meeting was adjourned, another half dozen
stopped to talk to Val, most with comments along the same
line. By the time the room had nearly emptied out, she was
feeling almost euphoric, though she knew her "victory" was
only temporary. Obviously, from the way Mrs. Plover and her
group left the room, stiffly and wordlessly except for an uncer-
tain, over-the-shoulder glance by the one who had nodded at
the conclusion of Val's remarks, the battle was far from over.
Val had just lucked out tonight, largely because of the unfortu-
nate analogy Mrs. Plover had chosen to use.

And then, as Val stood near the door waiting for Katherine,
she was pulled further back into reality. Earl Winters, who had
remained seated, watching the room slowly empty, finally stood
up and came over to her.

"Glad to see you here," she said as he stopped just in front
of her, "but from what you said the other night, I didn't think
you were much of a library user."

"To tell the truth, I'm not," he said. "Sally—that's my
wife—is the one who takes all the books out. At least, she's always getting some to read to our two kids." He grinned. "But
Jimmy, he's getting so he can read a lot of them himself. And
he's only four." There was an obvious glow of pride in his
words. Val had no trouble imagining him whipping out a hand-
ful of pictures, the way Dan had said the man did, and showing
his children off to anyone who would look or listen.

Val nodded. "I know how it is. That's the way I was when I

was that age. I was always reading to Millie—that's my younger sister—even if I had to sit on her to make her listen."

"Jimmy's the same way." There was an awkward silence as he hesitated, and then glanced around the almost empty room. "But the reason I came tonight is what's been happening to you. You know, the threats and things."

"I don't understand. Did you have second thoughts about my car being tampered with?"

"No, not that. It's just that, well, like I said, it *could* have happened accidentally, but it isn't likely. But that's not why I'm here."

"Why, then?"

"I just thought I'd keep an eye on everyone else, that's all. Just to see if it'd give me any idea who might be doing these things to you. You know, see if anyone looked suspicious." He shrugged, looking sheepish. "It seemed like a good idea when I thought of it."

"Did you see anyone who looked suspicious?"

He shook his head. "Just Martin, I guess. What did he want, anyway? I saw him drag you out into the hall, and you looked a little shook when you came back."

"Nothing new. He's just worried, that's all. Wants me to move out of my house until this guy is caught."

"Are you going to?"

"Hardly."

When she didn't volunteer anything else, he asked, "Have you thought of anyone who might have it in for you? For *you* rather than Martin, I mean?"

She shook her head. "Just Edna Plover and her group, and, as I said before, I'm sure that's not her style."

"You're sure you can't think of anyone else? Anyone at all?"

"Sorry."

He stood looking down at her, and, though his features were relatively well-controlled, Val noticed his fingers nervously flexing and straightening. Then, as Katherine Roberts and Sharon approached from the front of the room, he said, rapidly, "If you think of anyone, absolutely anyone, let me know."

Val watched puzzledly as he disappeared into the hall. Was it possible that *he* was being victimized, too? Or could *all* of Sandra's ex-boyfriends be getting notes or calls? And didn't *that* open up a whole new ball game!

"Trouble?" Katherine asked as she and her daughter stopped next to Val.

Val shook her head. "Not really, but I do think I'll give the sheriff a call when I get home," she said, and went on to mention her latest speculation.

Katherine was more skeptical than Sharon, but they both agreed it would be a good idea to let the sheriff know. Every little bit helps.

Then, as they left the room and walked down the hall past the other meeting rooms, Val noticed that the zoning board that Martin was supposed to have attended was just breaking up. Dan Richards, catching a glimpse of Val through the open door, hastily excused himself and hurried into the hall to meet Val.

"Have you heard from Marty?" he asked without preamble.

"Just before the meeting. He was here, and he said you were taking—"

"I know. He called me around supper time, said to get down here and hold Lichtenwalter's hand. He had 'personal business' to take care of. Did he tell you what it was all about when you saw him?"

"Not really," Val said, "but it wouldn't surprise me if he was out hiring another detective to guard me."

"Which might not be a bad idea. But was that what he talked to you about?"

"Actually, he didn't say anything about a bodyguard this time," she said, and went on to explain about Martin's offer of a temporary "safe house." She grimaced as she finished. "I can't say I cared much for the idea. Staying in a strange house by myself would hardly make me feel any safer."

"I don't blame you," Katherine said. "But just remember, if

you *would* like to move somewhere for a while, our offer is always open. You're welcome any time."

Sharon nodded her enthusiastic approval, but Dan caught her arm, bringing the group to a halt. "What house did Marty offer you?" Dan asked, his eyes narrowed.

Val shrugged. "He didn't say where it was. He just said he owned one that he normally rented out, but it was vacant right now."

Dan's frown deepened. "This so-called joke really *is* getting to him," he said. "Of all the places for him to want you to stay!"

"What's that supposed to mean?" Val asked. "Is there something wrong with the house?"

"Not for most people, no," he said, "but for you, for right now . . ." He shook his head wonderingly. "I don't know what's gotten into him, but that's the *last* place you should be spending any time. That house he rents out is the same one he and Sandra lived in when she was murdered."

He hurried from the Civic Center, plans whirling in his mind.

There was still hope! Despite the woman's stubbornness, there was hope. Now that he knew where the cat had been taken, there was hope.

But it would have to be done tonight, before the situation could get even more complicated, more out of control than it already was.

Somehow, regardless of all obstacles, it would have to be completed tonight . . .

Chapter 13

It was midnight, and Val was sitting at the lamp end of the couch, munching an occasional potato chip, her legs curled underneath her as she skimmed through one of the library's recent paperback acquisitions, an adventure fantasy by a woman who, according to the biographical blurb, lived near Hartford City, not more than fifty miles from Hazleton. Val would have to call her sometime soon and see if she would be interested in talking to a group at the library. And if she was, then Val of course would have to see if she could scare up a group who wanted to listen, and then try to talk Katherine and the board into turning loose a little petty cash as a speaker's honorarium. But it might be worth a try. There were at least a few people locally who had ambitions to write, if their repeated use of the library's *Writer's Market* was any indication. And it would be encouraging to them to know that not all writers lived in New York or California.

She was jotting down the name of the author and her home town in a small notebook when the phone shattered the silence.

She managed not to drop the pencil and notebook as she snatched the phone from the floor at the end of the couch. The joker again? For the last time? With the trace arranged for, they would have him.

"Yes? What is it?" Her voice was steady, though a little higher-pitched than normal.

"Val? This is Katherine—Katherine Roberts."

The instant Val heard the hesitant voice, totally unlike Katherine's normal brusqueness, the tingling apprehension in her stomach suddenly became a lump of lead. Her arms felt weak, and she had to breathe deeply and hold the air tightly in her lungs for a second before she could speak again.

"Yes," she said finally, "what happened? Is it Muldoon?"

"Yes," the other woman said, and then rushed on, the words stumbling over each other. "Someone apparently broke in. I was positive we had locked the back door, but when we looked— But whoever it was, he didn't actually *get* Muldoon."

"He's still there?" Val's heart was suddenly pounding with relief.

"No, he's not here, but—"

"Where, then? What happened?"

"I don't know. Let me explain, Val, please. You see, Sharon heard him—the one who broke in, I mean. She has the back bedroom on the second floor. She was just going to sleep when she heard something like a cat fight. She thought of Muldoon right away, and she ran downstairs, and the back door was ajar. She turned on the light in the back yard and started to call when he came shooting over the fence from the alley. She ran out and tried to catch him, but he got past her and ran around to the front of the house. And then she heard a car starting up in the alley and driving away. She—"

"All right," Val said, cutting Katherine off sharply, "I'll be over in a couple of minutes. If he's still in the neighborhood, maybe I can find him."

"Val, no! You can't—"

"I'll be over," she said flatly and slammed the receiver into its cradle as she jumped to her feet.

Swearing silently, he grimaced as, sliding out of his car, his injured leg scraped painfully against the underside of the steering wheel. Slamming the door angrily, he looked down at the rips in the fabric of his trousers. Pausing, he touched the leg lightly with his fingers, testing to see if the bleeding had stopped. What had gotten into the creature, for God's sake? He had gotten it out of the house with barely a sound, only its usual subdued, purring meow, but then, as he had approached his car and had taken his keys from his pocket, the animal had virtually exploded in a frenzy of claws and yowls.

Abruptly he shook his head. Ignoring the pain as the trouser leg rubbed harshly against the half-dozen ragged scratches, he hurried into the house. The pain, even the acidlike burning as he smeared iodine on the scratches, was nothing compared to the emotional turmoil that engulfed him. The entire world seemed to be collapsing around his head.

Again he swore bitterly, feeling his stomach churn and twist in anger and frustration. He should have left well enough alone! He should never have made that one final, desperate effort to shore up that fool's pitiful strength! He should simply have written Forster off as a lost cause and proceeded on his own! Then, at least, something *could* have been salvaged! But now—

"*No!*"

The strangled cry rasped from his throat, shattering the silence of the darkened house. He couldn't give up! That would be admitting defeat! It would be admitting that he was no better than that impotent fool Forster! And he *had* to be better than that!

He had to be!

Otherwise he was lost, totally and forever. Forster could go on hiding from reality as long as he lived, like a mindless ostrich with his head in the sands of his own useless world, but he could not! He did not have that luxury! He had to face reality— and conquer it! If he could not do that, then he was nothing, just as that fool Forster was nothing! He had to continue. Somehow, no matter what the cost to himself, he had to continue. He had no other choice.

There had to be a way, even now . . .

Chapter 14

Sprague Roberts, a robe thrown on hastily over his pajamas, made a lurching U-turn and pulled to the curb a few yards ahead of where Val was walking rapidly down the sidewalk, the can of cat crunchies rattling sporadically in her hand.

"Val, get in this car!" he called. "After what's happened, you can't just walk around out here like this!"

"No, thanks," she said. "You can keep an eye on me from the car if you want, but that's all."

"Please, Val, get in. Katherine is—"

"Sorry, Sprague, but no way." She held the can up and shook it loudly, looking in all directions as she did. "The sooner I look, the better chance I have of finding him. And don't worry," she added, taking the water pistol from the pocket of the dark zippered jacket she had thrown on over her sweater and jeans, "I'm more or less protected."

Sprague slumped back in the seat, apparently recognizing the steely tone in her voice. Val, putting the water gun back in her pocket, continued walking, moving more slowly now as she neared the Roberts' block. If Muldoon were anywhere within hearing, this *should* bring him out, she thought as she rattled the can once more—unless he's just too frightened by whatever happened.

Or unless whoever had taken him from the Roberts' house had somehow been able to catch him again.

She cut that thought off, unwilling—yet—to consider such possibilities. Pulling in her breath, she added a piercing whistle to the next rattle of the can, but the only response was a sudden flurry of barking from across the street.

As she reached the sidewalk in front of the Roberts' house, Sprague, who had been slowly paralleling her in his car, pulled hastily into the driveway, stopping directly across the sidewalk, blocking her path. At the same time, the front door of the house opened and Sharon came running out, followed more slowly by her mother. Sharon, like Val, was in jeans and sweater, while her mother was still in a bulky terry-cloth robe.

Sharon stumbled to a halt in front of Val. The girl's eyes were red from the tears that smudged her cheeks. They stood silently for a second, and then Sharon, her voice breaking, said, "I'm sorry, Miss Hamilton. I *tried* to catch him before he got out of the yard, but I couldn't. I just couldn't!"

Impulsively, Val reached out to the girl. "It's all right, Sharon. It wasn't your fault. It wasn't anyone's fault, except maybe mine for not taking this thing more seriously."

Sharon hesitated only a moment, and then she was in Val's arms. Val could hear the girl's quiet sobs, and somehow her open, honest reaction made it easier for Val to control her own emotions. At least, she thought, there was no stupid ass hovering around saying "don't get so worked up, it's *only* a cat."

"Don't worry about it," Val said softly. "Whoever broke in didn't get him. That's the important part. And once he calms down, we'll find him. Or he'll find us." She gave the can of crunchies an illustrative rattle behind the girl's back, then released her.

As Val looked up, she saw Katherine standing only a couple of feet behind Sharon. She brushed a hand through her daughter's blond hair and let it rest on her shoulder, squeezing gently. She looked at Val then. "Dan Richards will be here in a minute," she said. "He said he'd help you look, too."

"You called Dan?"

"Right after we called the sheriff's office," Katherine said, pulling her robe more tightly around her spare body. "Now let's go inside and wait until they get here. We could all use a little time to calm down—including Muldoon, no doubt."

Val smiled faintly and nodded. She looked back at Sprague, who still stood next to the open door of his car, as if ready to leap back in at a moment's notice. "You can relax," Val said. "I'm not going to run off—at least not for a few minutes."

He watched her warily for a moment before climbing back into the car long enough to pull it all the way into the drive. Then, following the others to the house and into the kitchen, he plugged in the coffee maker on the counter and started rummaging through the cabinets in search of the coffee itself.

"You didn't call Martin, did you?" Val asked as they settled down around the kitchen table.

"Of course not," Katherine said. "I thought the entire idea was to keep as much of this from him as we could."

Val nodded. "It is. But after tonight it won't be easy."

Dan arrived before the coffee was heated, and, while he was trying to find out precisely what had happened, a deputy arrived. He pulled a notebook from his uniform shirt pocket as Sprague ushered him into the kitchen.

"I understand you had a burglary here?" he said, not sounding overly interested.

"A break-in," Katherine said. "He must have gotten in through this door." She pointed at the kitchen door. "My daughter found it open."

The deputy—Harold Strang, if Val remembered correctly—only partially suppressed a bored sigh as he went to inspect the door. He shook his head as he looked at the lock. "Spring lock," he said. "Easiest thing in the world to open. Should have a deadbolt or a chain." He turned to the others, digging a ballpoint pen from his pocket to go with the notebook. "Now, do you have any idea what was taken? Have you made—"

He stopped abruptly as his eyes, in their bored inspection of the room, came across Val. He blinked, and the boredom vanished.

"Miss Hamilton?"

She nodded. "That's right."

"What are *you* doing here?"

"It was my cat that the so-called burglar took when he broke in. The only thing he took, apparently."

"But this—" The deputy looked around sharply, then back at

Val. "This *is* the Roberts' place. Isn't it? Mrs. Roberts, aren't you the one who called?"

"Yes, I called, and it's our house. But it's Miss Hamilton's cat. It's a long story, but we were taking care of him for her."

Deputy Strang blinked, and then hastily shoved his notebook and pen back in his pocket. "Can I use your phone?"

"Of course," Katherine said, pointing to where the instrument was mounted on the wall not far from the electric range.

The deputy glanced at Katherine as he hurried toward the phone. "You should've told me when you called, Mrs. Roberts," he said accusingly. "Mel wanted to be notified about anything having to do with Miss Hamilton, anything at all."

Before anyone could answer, he was dialing the phone and then explaining the situation to Sheriff Mel Lawrence. "He'll be over in a few minutes," the deputy said when he hung up. "I better just wait until he gets here. He wants to look over everything himself."

Over the deputy's protests, Dan and Val made a circuit of the block with the can of cat crunchies, but when Lawrence arrived, the searching came to an abrupt end.

"I'll handcuff the lot of you if I have to," he said tersely, his rounded face slightly flushed, "but no one is wandering around the streets looking for that cat tonight! I'm not taking *any* chances! And you, Miss Hamilton, had better take Mrs. Roberts up on her offer and stay the night here."

"But I have to—"

"I don't care *what* you have to do! You're not going to stay there alone tonight!" He glared at her. "I don't know what's going on around here, but I do know that the last time anything *like* it happened, there was a murder close behind! And *this* time, by God, I'm not making the same mistakes all over again!"

"All right!" Val snapped. "No one's blaming you for what happened to Sandra Forster! But unless you *do* handcuff both of us, Dan and I are going to take at least one more look around the neighborhood, and *I* am going to go home and make sure Muldoon can get in if he comes back when no one is there!"

The sheriff's jaw tightened, and Val could see the tendons in his neck stand out in sharp relief. After several seconds of angry silence, he turned to the deputy. "Get the fingerprint kit, since you forgot to bring it!" he snapped. "I'll call Dale and Barney and get them in to help."

"But they don't come on duty until—"

"I *know* when my deputies come on duty! Now move!"

As Strang, almost cowering, rushed out to his car, Lawrence picked up the phone and, in short terse commands, ordered his other two deputies to meet him at the Roberts' house immediately, he didn't care *what* he was interrupting. When he hung up, he stood silently, his back to everyone in the room. Then, slowly, he took in a deep breath and turned to face them.

"All right," he said, focussing on Val, "you haven't gotten any more calls since the one last night?"

She shook her head. "No."

"And if what happened tonight is any indication, you won't *be* getting any more." He grimaced. "It looks as if he decided to skip the rest of the preliminaries and get right down to business."

"But he didn't quite succeed," Val pointed out. "Muldoon got away."

"Which may mean nothing at all. Incidentally, I talked to Earl Winters and a couple of the others about that idea you had. You know, about all of Mrs. Forster's former boyfriends maybe getting threats of some kind. They all denied it."

"Naturally." Val glanced impatiently at her watch. "Now look, Sheriff, I told you, I am at least going to go back to my house long enough to make sure Muldoon's window is unlatched."

"His *window?*" Lawrence frowned at her.

Val explained about the tiny, swinging window. "It's too small for a human," she assured him, "and I always leave it unlatched if Muldoon is still outdoors when I have to leave for work. Now are you going to let me—"

"The sheriff is right, Val," Dan said. "You're better off here, at least for right now. But if you want to give me your keys, I'll run over and make sure the window is unlatched. All right? I'll even try to pack an overnight case for you, if you can tell me what you need."

"Thanks, Dan, but I—"

"Let him do it," Lawrence said. "I told you, the last thing I want is for you to be running around loose somewhere in the middle of the night."

Finally she gave in and handed Dan her keys. She told him where Muldoon's window was and what to bring back. "And grab my purse while you're at it," she finished. "It's probably on the desk in my office."

As Dan left, Val turned irritably to Lawrence. "You *are* going to let me go back in the morning to change clothes, aren't you?" she said, displaying her faded jeans and sweater. "These are comfortable enough, but I don't feel like wearing them to work. And I'll have to see if Muldoon made it back during the night. All right?"

"We'll see. Now about this business tonight—who knew where your cat was being kept?"

"Dan. And Martin. And whoever was listening to us at the library board meeting this evening. And whoever any of them told. And anyone who saw me bring him over here last week. Or saw me come to visit here yesterday morning."

"But Richards and Forster are the only ones you know of for sure?"

"If you want to put it that way, yes, but—"

"Have you talked to Forster this evening?"

"Not since the meeting. But he's the *victim* of all this! You certainly can't—"

"Mind if I use your phone again?" Without waiting for a reply, Lawrence began leafing through the phone book, hanging by a string from a hook next to the phone. Locating the number, he dialed. Silently, he listened for at least a full minute.

"No answer," he said, hanging up. "Where do you suppose

Forster could be at this time of night?" Lawrence asked, eyeing Val curiously.

"How should *I* know? Maybe he just isn't answering the phone at night. I can't say I'd blame him, considering what's been happening."

He shrugged. "Possible. I think you said Earl Winters was at your board meeting, too. Could *he* have overheard you?"

"Maybe. But you said you'd already talked to him this evening."

"Over two hours ago, not recently." He flipped through the phone book again and dialed. Apparently someone answered, because Lawrence mumbled a hasty, "Sorry, wrong number," and hung up.

"At least *he's* home," Lawrence said, turning back to Val. "Anyone else who might know about the cat's whereabouts?" When she didn't answer, he turned to Sharon Roberts. "What about you? Did *you* tell anyone? Anyone at school, for instance? Friends? Teachers?"

"No! Mother told me not to, and I didn't!"

He looked questioningly at Katherine Roberts, who nodded sharply. "If she says she didn't tell anyone, she didn't."

He stood, frowning silently at the floor for a time before looking up. "Mrs. Roberts, Mr. Roberts—are you *positive* the cat was taken intentionally? Couldn't it have been just a simple burglary? The door was left open for a quick retreat, and the cat got out?"

"But nothing was touched," Katherine said. "And a burglar wouldn't break into a house while people were in it, would he?"

Lawrence shrugged his beefy shoulders. "It happens."

Another five minutes of repetitive questioning produced nothing new, and then, shattering another of the recurrent silences that fell when Lawrence ran out of questions, the phone rang. Sprague Roberts, who had been leaning against the range next to the phone, jerked around and grabbed the receiver.

"Hello?"

His frown deepened as he listened. Then he held the receiver out to the sheriff. "For you. It's Dan Richards."

Lawrence snatched the phone from the man's hand. "Yes, Richards?"

He listened for several seconds. "All right," he said, the words clipped and rapid, "never mind picking up anything for Miss Hamilton. Come on back here. And thanks."

Abruptly he broke the connection with his finger and instantly began dialing. Silently, he waited, drumming his fingers on top of the range.

"What—" Val and Sharon both began, but Lawrence waved them to silence.

Finally, he spoke sharply into the phone. "Yes, Mrs. Dalton, this is Sheriff Mel Lawrence. Your supervisor informed you about the trace on— That's right, that's the number. Miss Valerie Hamilton's phone. A call just came through. Check your printout." He closed his eyes in a brief grimace of impatience. "Yes, Mrs. Dalton, check it *now*."

He continued to drum nervously on the range top as he waited. He looked over his shoulder at Val. "Our friend called while Richards was at your place. He was whispering something about not getting your cat but still getting you. But now *we've* got *him!* As soon as that— Yes, Mrs. Dalton?"

He turned his full attention to the phone. "You're positive? And whose number is that?" His eyes widened as he listened. He had started to jot down the information in his notebook, but now he stopped. "You're absolutely sure? There's no chance your computer could've made a mistake? Crossed a wire?" Another pause. "All right, thank you. No, leave the trace on for the time being. I don't want to take any chances. Thank you."

As he hung up, he turned to face the others. While his back had been turned, his frown had changed to a faint but self-satisfied grin. "Maybe you'll be able to sleep in your own bed tonight after all, Miss Hamilton," he said. "It looks very much like we've got our friend nailed down."

"Who is it?" everyone asked in a disjointed chorus.

Lawrence's grin widened a bit. "We can't be a hundred percent sure, of course, but whoever it is, he made that last call of his from the telephone of Mr. and Mrs. Wallace Jeskie."

It was working!

Barely an hour ago, defeat had been a near certainty, yet now he was on the verge of success!

His victory might not be as complete as he had once hoped, but it would be a victory! There would be vengeance, with or without Forster's help, of that much he was positive. And if Forster himself could somehow still be prodded into action even now . . .

Yes, it was working, and it had been so simple, so incredibly, elegantly simple! Forster, that plodding fool, would never have thought of it, not in a thousand years! A simple phone call, a few dozen words in all, was all it had taken.

And now, if his luck held up, the final act would, at last, be under way.

Chapter 15

The evidence found in Wally Jeskie's desk in his den was seemingly conclusive. There was, first and foremost, a notebook with some pages torn out. The top page of the ones remaining held indentations that matched perfectly the lettering in the note that had been attached to Muldoon's collar. The same drawer also held a tape of Sandra's voice, obviously the one used to record over Val's voice on the tape Dan Richards had made. And in another drawer of the same desk were several pieces of inexpensive but distinctive jewelry, apparently part of what Thelma had inherited from Sandra, although Thelma, between glances of surprised admiration at her husband, refused to identify them as such.

Lawrence stopped by to give Val and the others the news personally and to tell Val she could safely return home. "Either Jeskie was putting on a terrific act all these years, making believe he didn't believe Thelma's ravings, or else he was finally converted—with a vengeance."

"But he doesn't admit that he did it all?" Val asked.

"Not yet. But he will, don't worry. It was all right there in his desk, everything we'll need. It couldn't be any plainer."

"What will happen to him?"

Lawrence shrugged. "Depends a lot on whether you and Forster want to press any kind of charges. And just how hundred-percent-sure we can be that he didn't have anything to do with Sandra Forster's murder."

"You certainly don't think—"

Again Lawrence shrugged. "Anything's possible. Not likely, but possible. Anyway, you don't have anything to worry about.

Whatever happens down the road, he's locked up for the night. And even if someone puts up bail—and I'll bet that wife of his does, fast! She was looking at him like she just discovered a brand new Lone Ranger right under her nose. Anyway, even if he gets out tomorrow or the day after, we'll keep a close eye on him, so you won't have any more trouble."

Dan offered to drive Val home, but she insisted on walking. "It's only three or four blocks," she said, "and I want to take another shot at luring Muldoon out of the bushes." She rattled the can of cat crunchies as she picked it up from the kitchen table. "You *did* remember to open his window in the basement, didn't you?" she asked.

Dan nodded. "I'd just gotten it unlatched when the phone rang."

"Val?" Katherine, still in her terry-cloth robe, approached Val apologetically. "If he isn't back by morning, I'll run a special announcement in the paper. With a picture, if you have one."

Val started to protest the favor, but she stopped abruptly. "It's not your fault he's missing," she said, "and I don't want you to even think anything like that. But I *will* accept your offer. *If* he hasn't found his way home by morning, I'll bring a picture down to your office."

"And I can put up reward posters or something like that at school," Sharon put in with a mixture of sadness and enthusiasm. "And talk to all the kids about him. Someone's sure to find him."

Val thanked them all, giving Sharon a comforting hug when she saw what looked like new tears beginning to form in the corner of one eye. "I'm sure you're right. Now that no one's trying to hurt him, he'll be okay."

Despite Val's protests, Dan insisted on walking home with her. They found no sign of Muldoon, but two dogs answered Val's whistles, and one pair of bedroom drapes were parted suspiciously as they walked past, whistling and rattling.

At her front door, she took the keys from her jacket pocket and, as silently as she could, unlocked it. She wouldn't want to scare him off with an inadvertent clink of the keys if he were lurking about the yard somewhere. As she swung the door open and listened, there was no sound from inside the house.

Val looked up at Dan, reluctant to enter the empty house alone, not because of any fear but simply because of the emptiness and the silence. And for a moment she thought: *If only he could stay, just to hold me* . . .

Harshly, she forced the thought away. An empty house and a missing cat are *not* sufficient reason for thinking about marriage or any other arrangement.

Then he was leaning down, and their lips were meeting. She started to put her arms around his waist, but the rattle of the cat food can, still in her right hand, stopped her, and they both laughed self-consciously as they stepped apart.

"Anything I can do for you?" he asked quietly.

She shook her head. "Just keep an eye out for stray cats as you walk back to your car. And thanks for walking with me."

They kissed again, silently this time, and a little sadly, and then he was hurrying across the lawn and turning to wave as he reached the sidewalk.

Val watched until he was out of sight beyond the hedges two doors away, and then, with more reluctance than she liked to admit, even to herself, she forced herself to enter the empty, silent house.

He waited in the darkness, hardly daring to breathe, so loud did the intake of air seem to his hypersensitive ears.

For nearly an hour, he waited in the musty darkness as her footsteps moved from room to room overhead, as she repeatedly went first to the back door and then the front to try to summon the cat. Nervously, he glanced at the faintly luminous dial of his watch, wondering how long until the first light of dawn.

But finally, when he had almost begun to despair, he heard her walk to the bedroom. Holding his breath, he could hear the springs creak as she lowered herself onto the bed. He could

*even, he imagined, hear the rustle of the sheets as she slid be-
tween them.*

*Slowly, stealthily, the crepe soles of his shoes barely whisper-
ing on the steps, he made his way up from the basement. Then,
making each movement individually and silently, he crept the
short length of the hall and across the kitchen to the back door.
With infinite care, he slid the chain from the latch and lowered
it.*

*With equal caution, he retreated to the head of the basement
stairs and turned, closing the door until there remained only the
narrowest of cracks, just enough to give him a sliver of a view
of the shadowy hall and the door to her bedroom a dozen feet
away.*

He waited.

Soon it would begin.

*Would Forster respond? Or would he be forced to take mat-
ters into his own hands?*

But whatever happened, it would soon begin.

And five years of tortured waiting would be over.

Soon . . .

Chapter 16

Val's eyes snapped open in the darkness, her heart suddenly racing.

Had she been asleep and only dreamed the sound, or—

Muldoon? Could she have heard his basement window clicking shut behind him all the way up here?

She sat up abruptly, throwing back the covers and snapping on the lamp on the nightstand. For a moment she sat on the edge of the bed, blinking against the glare of the light, and then she was shrugging into the heavy, woolen robe that lay in a heap on the foot of the bed. Impatiently, she jammed her feet into an aging but comfortable pair of house slippers.

Hastily knotting the belt of the robe about her waist, she hurried around the bed toward the door to the hall. She was halfway through the door, reaching for the hall light switch on the opposite wall next to the door to her office, when she heard:

"Please, Miss Hamilton, don't panic."

Val gasped, almost screaming, as the hushed voice came at her from the shadows of the hall.

Instinctively, she started to back through the door into the bedroom, but she stopped as she remembered there was no lock on the door. And where, for God's sake, had she tossed her jacket, with the water pistol still in the pocket?

"Don't be afraid," the voice came again, and this time, her hand gripping the doorframe, she looked toward the sound. "It's me, Earl Winters."

As he spoke, she was able to make out his solid, muscular form standing motionless in the door between the hall and the kitchen, barely two yards away. Both hands were extended in her direction, but the palms were down, in a keep-calm gesture, not a threatening one. He was dressed in dark clothing, including what looked like a black turtleneck. His tightly curling black hair was tangled, as if he had been constantly, nervously running his fingers through it.

Val could feel her heart pounding, but she managed to keep her voice steady as she said, "All right, Mr. Winters, I won't panic if you'll tell me how you got in here."

She heard him swallow, an exaggerated gulping sound in the otherwise breathless silence. He was, she realized, as nervous as she was herself.

"Someone gave me a key," he said.

"What? *Who* gave you a key? And why?"

"That's what *I* would like to find out."

A trembling pause, and then: "You aren't the person who's been calling me? The one who put the note on my cat's collar and all the rest?"

He shook his head sharply. "No! *He's* been calling *me!*"

"Who was it? Could it have been Wally Jeskie?"

"It could have been anyone. But why do—"

"Because he was arrested for making the calls and everything a couple of hours ago."

He let his breath out in a whoosh of relief, but then, as if having second thoughts, he swore. "You said he was arrested a couple of hours ago. Do you know exactly what time it was?"

"A little before two. Probably closer to one-thirty."

"You're sure?"

"It's about the only time I *am* sure about. The sheriff came by to tell us, and I remember looking at the clock on the wall and thinking that, even if I got home and to sleep right away, I'd only have five hours' sleep, since I get up at seven." She managed a nervous grin. "Looks like I'm not going to get even that much."

"It wasn't Jeskie," Winters said flatly. "Whoever it was, he called me just after two."

A new lump of lead formed in Val's stomach. "You want to

talk about it?" she asked, somehow keeping her voice steady and, she hoped, soothing.

"Very much." He nodded emphatically.

"In the living room? Where we can at least sit down?" And be close to my jacket and, I hope, the water pistol, she added to herself.

He nodded again. "But no lights."

"Whatever you say."

"And close the door to the bedroom, so no light gets out."

Slowly, she pulled the door shut behind her. The light thinned to a crack and then vanished except for a faint sliver at the bottom of the door. Winters' massive form had faded almost completely into the darkness of the hall. The only light now was coming dimly through the curtained living-room windows.

Slowly, making no sudden movements, Val walked down the short hall and through the arch into the living room. In the dim light she could see her jacket on the arm of the couch at the far end. But in the near darkness, could she—if she had to—find the pocket and get the water pistol out? And would the ammonia in it *really* work? The odor, she knew from when she had filled the pistol, was really horrible, but was it enough to actually incapacitate someone? Katherine had insisted that it was, but . . .

She eased herself down on the couch near the jacket. Winters stood looking down at her from four or five feet away, just beyond the end of the coffee table.

"You still haven't told me *why* you're here," she said, letting her left hand drop with seeming casualness on the jacket.

"I've been ordered to kill you."

Her whole body twitched, as if the words had been an electric shock. She felt weak. The fingers of her left hand, already probing the shapeless lump of her jacket, began to move more rapidly.

She opened her mouth to speak, but for what seemed like an eternity, no words emerged. Finally, when she had control of her throat and tongue again, she asked, in barely a whisper, "Why? Who?"

He lowered his eyes as he shook his head. "I don't know."

He glanced toward the windows. Despite the shadows, the street seemed to Val to be a haven of light compared to this room.

"But whoever it is," Winters went on, "he said that he would be watching, to make sure I did it. That's why I don't want the lights on, so he can't see that we're just talking."

"But I don't understand. If he— Why haven't you gone to the police?"

"He warned me not to. He said he would kill Jimmy if I did. Or if I didn't go through with it and kill you."

"Jimmy? Your son?"

"Yes."

She swallowed, realizing that she must have poked every inch of her jacket without finding a lump that would indicate she had found the water pistol.

"Are you going to do it?" she asked, surprised that her voice didn't at least tremble.

"I don't *want* to. What I *want* to do is find out who it is that wants me to kill you. If I can do that, then I *can* go to the police. That's why I was at the meeting last evening, why I called you Sunday. That's even why I sabotaged your car, fixed it so it would die after a mile or two, and I'd have an excuse to talk to you somewhere that we wouldn't be seen."

"But if you can't find out who it is? Will you—will you kill me?"

"I don't know." He looked directly at her for a moment, and then lowered his eyes to the carpet at her feet again. "I honest to God don't know!"

And then, suddenly, a new shock lanced through her. Her fingers, still entwined in the jacket, twitched and stiffened. She remembered. She had taken the water pistol out of the jacket and dropped it, along with her keys, on the small bookcase in the hall, just inside the front door.

Her heart pounding even harder, she looked past Winters' shadowy form, trying to gauge the distance, trying to get her frozen mind to come up with a few plausible words that would allow her to get past Winters and into the hall.

But then, as her eyes probed the shadows behind him, she became aware of a deeper, solider shadow just beyond the arch, in the hall. She hadn't thought her heart could pound any harder or faster than it already was, but somehow it did.

She held her breath as she saw a shadowy hand snaking into the room toward the light switch. If Winters didn't see or hear—

Then, abruptly, she thought: But *this* must be the one who *ordered* Winters to kill me! Who else could it be?

For a fraction of a second, the turmoil in her mind kept her silent, but then, "Earl! Look out! There's someone—"

As Winters spun around, the room erupted into blinding brightness from the overhead light.

Her eyes ached from the sudden brilliance and her eyelids involuntarily shuttered down. Then, as the ache faded and full vision returned, she gasped in sudden, shocked relief.

Winters stood frozen, his back toward her now. And facing him, standing in the arch to the hall, was Martin Forster. He was tieless, his dark jacket smudged with dirt and dust in a dozen places, his dark hair as much a tangle as Winters'.

And in Martin's trembling hand, pointed directly at Winters, was a gun.

"Martin! I don't know how you—"

"What are you doing here, Winters?" Martin asked, his voice as unsteady as his hand. "How did you get in?"

As he spoke, he brought his other hand around to help support the gun in a trembling parody of the way TV policemen cover a suspect. Perspiration beaded his face. The tendons on the backs of his hands stood out as if the muscles were fighting desperately against each other.

And his face was a mask of total confusion.

From his position behind Martin Forster's eyes, he watched. "Kill him!" he whispered into Forster's ears. "Kill him before he fills her mind with even more lies! Kill him before he kills her, *the way he killed Sandra! Kill him* now! *Take our revenge! Redeem us,* now!"

But the finger that curled rigidly around the trigger could only tremble and shake. Both hands together could not hold the gun steady. And he could feel Forster's stomach rebelling. He could feel Forster's mind fighting desperately against what it saw and heard, just as it had five endless years before, threatening once again to retreat into unreality and blot out the truth that seemed ready, literally, to drown him.

And he realized, finally and irrevocably, what he should have known all along: The spineless, incompetent fool was simply unable to do it! He had been unable to protect her then, and he was unable to protect her now! He had given him the chance, given him every chance he could possibly give him, and still he was failing!

Once again, he was left with only one choice, one course of action if he were to survive with even a shred of self-respect.

Chapter 17

"Martin!" Val said. "Thank God you're here! But *what's going on?*"

Then, as she started to move away from Winters and the couch, toward the windows on the other side of the room, Martin straightened. The trembling stopped in the same instant, as if it had been cut off by a switch. The gun was suddenly steady, his arms and hands pointing it rigidly, as if they were extensions of the metal in the gun itself.

"You didn't think I'd let you get away with it, did you, Winters?" His voice, too, was steady, and there was, shockingly, a faint smile forming on his lips. All hesitancy and uncertainty were gone, replaced by a cold and frightening intensity.

"I'll call the sheriff," Val said. She started to move past Martin, who had moved a couple of steps into the room from the hall. "The phone is plugged in in the bedroom."

"No!" Martin snapped. "Just stay where you are!"

"But Martin—"

"I said, no!"

"Martin, *what* is going on? Are you all right?"

He didn't look at her, but his lip curled in a sneer as he answered in a mocking voice. "Yes, I'm all right." He laughed. "For the first time in five years, I'm all right! Or I *will* be in just a few minutes." The gun, still unwavering, pointed directly at Winters' chest. "As soon as I take care of some unfinished business."

"Martin, please! I don't know what you think was happening here, but Earl was being forced to—"

Martin's harsh laugh cut her short. "Of course he was! I

heard that insane story he was telling you! And you actually believed him?" He shook his head incredulously.

"But why else would he— Martin, I don't understand!" Val almost screamed the words.

"I'm sure you don't, but our friend Mr. Winters here knows." Martin punctuated his statement with a jabbing motion of the gun, causing Winters to wince. "Don't you, Mr. Winters? You know what's coming—and why! Just because that other fool was powerless to do anything to you, don't think that I'm the same!"

Martin shook his head, snorting derisively. "No, don't think for a single second that I'm the same coward that's been hiding his head in the sand for the past five years! He's gone now— gone for good! *I'm* the one you have to deal with now. But you won't have to deal with me for long, Mr. Winters, don't worry about that! Not long at all."

Martin made another jabbing motion with the gun, as if he wanted to skewer Winters on it. "Only a few minutes, Mr. Winters, only a few minutes. They won't make up for all those years, but they'll have to do."

"Martin—" Val began, but he cut her off sharply.

"Keep out of this," he snapped. "Don't interfere in something you don't—something you *can't* understand!"

In the brief silence that followed, Winters spoke for the first time since Martin had appeared. His voice held a note of bafflement. "*You're* the one who's been calling me," he said. "*You're* the one who ordered me to kill her!"

"Martin!" Val gasped the name, realizing suddenly that Winters was right. "Why, Martin? Why would you want me—"

"I told you, keep out of this! It doesn't concern you! It's between this murderer and me!"

"You order him to *kill* me, and you say it doesn't *concern* me?"

"I never intended for him to actually *harm* you, for God's sake!" he snapped impatiently, as if reprimanding a backward child. "Can't you even see *that* much? I was only trying to give that idiot Forster another chance—a chance to *redeem* himself!"

He broke off, shaking his head violently again. "It doesn't matter! Forster failed, so it doesn't matter any more! But *I* won't fail!"

Val steadied herself with one hand on the back of the recliner chair next to her, trying to keep the room from spinning insanely around her. Finally, it came to rest.

"All right, Martin," she said in as calm and soothing a voice as she could manage, and at the same time she began to move slowly away from the chair, trying to move wide around Martin toward the arch to the hall just behind him. "We have to call the sheriff. Now I'm going to—"

"No!" Martin's voice was almost a snarl. "I didn't let Forster ruin it, and I won't let *you* ruin it!"

"You don't want to hurt *me,* Martin," she said, barely able to keep her voice from breaking as she continued to move, easing herself sideways toward the hall now. "Do you? No, I know you don't. You've been trying to protect me. You even hired someone to—"

"*Forster* hired that detective, not me! Can't you *understand,* for God's sake?"

"All right," she said, avoiding the use of his name, "all right. I understand." She was almost even with him now. Another yard and she would be past him to the hall. "It's all right," she repeated, unable to think of anything else that would be safe. "It's—"

"Get back there!" he half shouted, his eyes darting back and forth between herself and Winters. "I told you, don't meddle in something you don't understand!"

Then, when she didn't move instantly to comply, he half turned and grasped her arm with fingers that bit deep into the flesh of her upper arm.

"I said *get back there!* The sheriff has nothing to do with this!"

Violently, she was flung backward, sprawling over the arm of the chair and into the seat with a force that rocked the chair on its base.

And in that instant, while Martin had his full attention on Val, Winters lunged forward, his hand slapping at the gun, sending it spinning across the room and crashing to the floor below the windows. Then the same hand, doubled into a fist, swung backhanded against the side of Martin's head, sending him reeling against the wall. A moment later, before Val had a chance to do more than make an abortive effort to struggle out of the chair, Winters had snatched up the gun.

He stood, his back to the window, breathing heavily. His eyes met Val's for an instant, and she thought she saw sadness, not triumph, but then they shifted to Martin, who was struggling to his feet, one hand gripping the edge of the archway, the other pressed to the side of his head.

Heavily, Winters moved toward Martin, grasped his arm with his free hand, and almost literally threw him into the living room, sending him floundering against the couch. As Martin steadied himself, Val saw a ragged streak of blood starting just above his temple and running halfway down his cheek. His eyes were glazed, but slowly they cleared.

Winters, still breathing heavily, looked again at Val, still sprawled in the chair. He glanced toward the windows and slipped the gun into his jacket pocket, but his hand remained in the pocket as well. His eyes, as they met hers, again seemed to soften into sadness, but they hardened as, straightening his broad shoulders, he shifted slightly to face Martin.

"All right," Winters said, enunciating the words carefully, "now we'll see who has to deal with who."

Martin, unsteadily erect, flinched at the words and then looked angrily at Val. "Do you realize what you've done? You've killed us both! Do you realize that?" His voice was a high-pitched mixture of anger and terror.

For a moment, Val's own anger blocked out the panic that she felt. "I only wanted to call the sheriff!" she said, her voice trembling. "You looked as if you were going to shoot him in cold blood!"

Martin shook his head incredulously, wincing at the sudden motion. "Don't you understand? Even now? *He* killed Sandra! I *saw* him!"

"But if you saw him, why didn't you tell the police? It was five years ago! Why—"

"Because that other spineless fool refused to face reality! *I* had to force him to see the truth!"

Fearfully, she turned toward Winters. "It's not true. Is it?"

For a moment, just a moment, his features brightened, as if he had been granted a sudden reprieve, but then they clouded. "I'm sorry, Miss Hamilton. I really am. But I don't have any choice." He scowled at Martin. "*He* saw to that!"

"Then you *did* kill Sandra?"

The scowl faded, and his voice took on a matter-of-fact tone. "She killed my son," he said. "It was only fair that she died, too."

"But your son is still alive! You told me—"

He shook his head sharply. "Not Jimmy! It was the abortion!"

Suddenly it came clear in Val's mind. The abortion *had* been to blame for Sandra's death, but not in the way Thelma had thought. It had been the father, not Martin Forster, who had killed her.

"Pull the drapes," Winters said. His hand was still in the jacket pocket, gripping the gun tightly.

Val pushed herself out of the chair and stood unsteadily erect for a second. Oddly, she felt calm despite the fact that her heart was pounding so strongly that she was sure the front of her robe must be pulsing in rhythm to its beat. If he took them somewhere, they would have to go past the bookcase in the hall —and the water pistol. Even now there might be a chance, a small chance.

Keeping one eye on Winters, she pulled the drapes. She was only a few feet from the hall. If she could—

Suddenly, from the far end of the darkened hall, came a rattling crash, thunderously loud in the tense silence. Winters spun around as if someone had jerked him with an invisible rope.

Without a word, he raced into the hall, searching frantically for the source of the sound.

And in that same instant, a fraction of a second after the sound, Val darted into the hall barely a foot behind Winters. Reacting automatically, not thinking past the next five seconds of her own survival, she grabbed blindly at the top of the bookcase in the hall. Her hand struck the keys, sending them clattering to the floor, but then her fingers closed over the water pistol.

Hearing the keys fall to the floor, Winters lurched to a halt and started to turn toward her. His hand was still in his pocket, but he was bringing it out.

Not bothering to aim, Val brought the water pistol up, squeezing the trigger spasmodically. The ammonia spurted from the barrel, spraying across the intervening three or four feet and splattering on Winters' sweater on his stomach and chest. His hand emerged from the pocket, the barrel of the gun snagging for an instant on the corner of the pocket, and then he was raising it. She squeezed the trigger again, and another spray hit his sweater, higher on his chest, just under his chin, and she was almost screaming, wanting to close her eyes so she wouldn't see Winters' gun as it came the rest of the way up and he pulled the trigger.

Then the stench hit her.

The hand holding the gun continued to come up, but the gun was no longer being pointed at her. The hand that held the gun and then the other grasped at the sweater, and Winters' face contorted. His mouth opened in a fishlike sucking motion, and he began to gasp and cough.

The gun clattered to the floor, and Val, holding her breath against the choking, eye-searing fumes, paused only long enough to snatch it up before she spun around and, fumblingly, frantically, got the front door open and stumbled outside into the cool, fresh air.

Then, as Winters, having clawed and torn the ammonia-soaked sweater off, leaned weakly against the open door, silence fell—except for a series of familiar sounds that floated

down the hall from the direction of the kitchen. First, there was
the distinctive sonaring meow of Muldoon, and then the sound
of his claws as they scrabbled to dislodge the lid from the can
of crunchies he had knocked noisily to the floor a few seconds
before. And finally, there was the sound of contented
crunching.

Val's eyes filled with tears, not all from the now-dissipating
ammonia.

In the two hours after Val, still out of breath from both
nerves and ammonia fumes, called Dan and Sheriff Lawrence,
the entire story came out, starting with Winters' defiant admis-
sion that he had killed Sandra Forster because of the abortion,
"because she murdered my child!"

Val, having witnessed the confrontation between Martin and
Earl Winters, had guessed much of it and had realized that, except for Winters' jimmying of the choke on her car in Arlen's
parking lot that one night, Martin had been responsible for everything that had happened. Only a few details came as news,
such as how and when he had gotten the house keys from her
purse to have them duplicated, how he had kept Sandra's keys
to Thelma's house and had used them to steal the jewelry and
to make that last phone call and plant the evidence against
Wally, and how, on a visit to Milwaukee a year before, he had
been so impressed with her resemblance to Sandra that he had
determined, then and there, to somehow lure her to Hazleton so
he could "re-create" Sandra and everything leading up to her
murder in order to give "that fool Forster" a second chance, an
opportunity to "redeem himself and make it possible for us to
hold our heads up again."

Even so, it was eerily unsettling, particularly in the prosaic
surroundings of Sheriff Lawrence's small, dingy office, to hear
Martin talk about himself as if about a total stranger—and a
hated stranger, at that.

"He was there in plenty of time to save her, but he *didn't!*"
he grated at one point, cursing "Forster" violently. "He just
spied on her—through an opening in the drapes, for God's sake,

like a common peeping Tom! He saw her and Winters, and he thought: 'I knew it! She *hasn't* changed! Everything she's done is a fraud! Her marriage to me, the threats, the calls, even the cat—they're all just part of some scheme! And now she and her accomplice are there, together, making even more of a fool of me!' "

He broke off, fighting to keep the tears of anger from his eyes. "He couldn't see what was right before his eyes! He couldn't *see* the truth until the fingers closed around her throat! And even then, he did nothing! *Nothing!* Even when he saw Sandra killed before his very eyes, heard her gasping and strangling—even then, he did *nothing!* He was too much of a coward to save her! He was even too much of a coward to *remember his own failure!*"

And later in his bitter, rambling monologue, "For five *years* he did nothing! And *I could* do nothing! Until I saw this woman, this Valerie Hamilton, and in her I saw our salvation. But even after I managed to bring her here, he failed again— failed at every step! Even with everything I did—" He snorted derisively, angrily. "Get her to actually marry him? Not in a thousand years! But I should have known. I should have known! But in spite of him—in spite of his cowardice and stupidity, in spite of everything, I almost won. I almost won . . ."

The sun was still below the horizon when Val and Dan emerged from the sheriff's office and walked slowly across the street to the small parking lot in the courthouse square, but the sky had shaded from black to dark blue, and some high, wispy clouds were already catching the first reddish-purple rays of dawn. As they crossed the glisteningly damp strip of grass between sidewalk and curb, Val zipped her jacket against the chilly air. The streetlights had just gone out, but the stoplights on the other side of the square still blinked red in two directions and yellow in two instead of going through their daytime sequence of green, yellow, and red. The only sign of life was Avery's Cafe, a small lunch counter across the street to the north of the square, where Bill Avery, a freshly starched apron over his flannel shirt and Levi's, was getting ready for the breakfast trade, which would start in a few minutes.

"Let's stop," Val said, indicating Avery's. "Barely escaping with one's life makes one hungry. Besides, I want to pick up a reward."

"Reward? For whom? Not for me, certainly. I haven't been that much help."

"No, not for you. Although I appreciate all that you *have* done, such as it is. Not to mention your proposals, which are always good for the ego." Grinning, she paused on the sidewalk and, on tip toes, managed to reach his jaw, rough with twenty-four hours' worth of blond, almost invisible stubble.

"I have your permission to continue with them, then?" he asked, leaning down to return the kiss properly.

A muffled "Of course" moved her lips against his.

Reluctantly, he released her. "I thought you said the reward wasn't for me. That felt pretty much like a reward to me."

"That wasn't a reward. That was fun."

He laughed, taking her hand as they detoured across the corner of the square toward the cafe. "All right, then, who *is* the reward for?"

"Isn't it obvious? It's for the *real* hero of the night. The one who totally fouled up Martin's last-ditch plan, and then saved my neck and Martin's, too." Her grin widened as they pushed open the door to the cafe. "Someone who would, I'm sure, really appreciate about a quarter of a pound of good, raw hamburger."

And he did, so much so that he didn't make a single, sonaring sound the whole two minutes it took him to gobble it down.